A Powerless World

Book 3

When the Pain is Gone

P.A. Glaspy

Published by Vulpine Press in the United Kingdom in 2017

Cover by Claire Wood

ISBN: 978-1-910780-72-5

www.vulpine-press.com

For Jim, my husband, my confidante, my cheerleader, and my best friend. I could not have done this without you.

Since our group has grown so much, here's a quick breakdown of the players up to this point in the story. If anyone is confused, hopefully this will help.

Cast of Characters

At the Farm

Russ, Anne, and Rusty Mathews – this is their story, told from Anne's point of view. Rusty is fifteen years old.

Bob, Janet, and Ben Hopper – best friends of the Matthews, sharing their journey. Ben is fifteen years old.

Monroe and Millie Warren – Janet's aunt and uncle, owners of the farm. Monroe is an Army vet who served in Vietnam.

Brian Riggins – the Mathews' next-door neighbor; smart guy, so they brought him with them.

Marietta Sampson – former customer of Russ; close friend of Brian; included at Brian's request.

Sean and Kate Scanlin – found by Russ and Brian on a scouting mission, picked up on the way to the farm. Two daughters: Tara, ten years old; Katlyn, eight years old. Sean can make moonshine. Kate is an LPN (licensed practical nurse).

Luke and Casey Callen – friends of the Scanlins who lived close to the farm. Casey has a huge canning setup. Brought to the farm with their camper.

Mike Thomas – ran into the Scanlins while hunting for food for his group of neighbors; brought the Scanlins into their group; machinist, former Marine.

Ryan and Bill Lawton – brothers, neighbors of Mike. Landscapers by trade. Bill was killed by marauders

Pete and Sara Raines – neighbors of Mike and the Lawtons. One son, Tony, thirteen years old. Sara is a teacher. Pete was killed by marauders.

Lee Roush – neighbor of Mike, the Lawtons, and the Raines. Two kids: Aiden, nine years old; Moira, six years old. He's a carpenter. Wife Jackie never made it home from work when the EMP hit.

Matt and Nick Thompson – lived next door to the Warrens. When everything went down, Monroe brought them to stay at the farm, as their parents were in Memphis visiting family. Matt is seventeen years old; Nick is sixteen years old.

Jim and Charlotte Dotson – live close to the farm. Charlotte is disabled; Jim is retired and an avid hunter. Two adult daughters, Carrie and Ashley. Ashley is divorced with a daughter, Shannon, fifteen years old. Carrie is a nurse.

At the Sheriff's Office

Tim Miller – deputy; high school friend of some of the marauders (Alan's crew).

Gary Burns – sheriff.

Angie Hale – mayor.

Marauders

Les's Crew – Les, Joe, Mac, Ray, Junior, and Dave. These are the original scavengers from the Matthews' neighborhood in Book 1. They turned up again in the area vacated by Mike and his neighbors. Joe and Mac died there.

Alan's Crew – Alan, Rich, and Steve. They have made a run through an area not too far from the farm. Currently squatting at the Callen place.

Jay and Clay Glass – from town close to the farm. Have spent their time begging for food and supplies; live with their mother, Rhonda. Jay was killed by Ryan, in retribution for Bill's death.

Chapter 1

Alan and his crew had driven back to the Callen place for lack of another option. Steve had been in Alan's ear all the way there, when he could make himself heard over Rich's wailing.

"We can't stay there anymore, Al. You told those guys where we were holed up. The sheriff will be looking for us there. We need to load up and light out."

"I know. I know, *alright*? First thing is to get him took care of." He motioned with his head to the back of the truck. "Either we get him fixed up or I'm gonna fix him for good. He's driving me nuts with that caterwauling. *Shut up back there*!" He turned as he yelled it and the look on his face had Rich reducing the volume of his painful sounds to a quiet whimper. When they got to the house, they helped Rich get inside where he fell in a heap on the kitchen floor.

"Al, man, you gotta get me to a doctor or something. I think I'm bleedin' to death!" Rich was covered in blood down the right side of his body. Steve had taken his shirt off and given it to Rich to apply pressure to the side of his head where his right ear had been. One of Bill's shots had taken the ear off, leaving a bloody mess in its place.

"Sure Rich. Just where would you like me to take you? Ya reckon the minor emergency clinic is open? You know, the one right next to the sheriff's office? We should just go on into town right now. I bet those folks have been going to work every day, even though there's no electricity, which they need for *everything* they do. You're such an idiot! There ain't no more doctor's offices or clinics. Besides, you think they wouldn't tell the sheriff next door that someone was there with a gunshot wound? We'll just have to see if we can find something to wrap it up with for now. Steve, go look in the bathroom, see if those assholes left any bandages, since they sure as hell didn't leave much of anything else. And get him something for the pain so he'll shut the fuck up for five minutes! God knows we've got plenty of that kind of stuff."

Steve walked toward the bathroom, shaking his head and mumbling to himself about it being a bad idea to have come back there and that they were getting busted for sure if they stayed. Al could hear him but chose not to respond just then. He was digging through the drugs they had looted from other homes. He spied what he was looking for, pulled the bottle out of the pile, and handed two to Rich.

"Here. Swallow these Vicodin. They'll ease your pain, and give my head a break from your screechin'."

Rich took the pills and laid down on his left side. Steve came back with an old sheet he was ripping into strips. "No bandages, but I found this sheet. We can make a pad for the ear—well, what's left of it—and wrap some around his head to hold it on. Let me get some booze to put on it, see if we can clean it up some."

Steve went to work on Rich, which of course made Rich start screaming again. Al went out on the porch, smoked some meth, and zoned out. He thought about the day's events. *Things didn't go good at all. In fact, it was a pretty shitty day. And we still don't know what they have in there ... except that one of those guys is a hell of shot. Hit that stupid kid dead center in the head. That's what happens when you're a dumbass and you stand there like that when there's people shooting. I'm surprised either of them lived as long as they have since the shit went down. But Steve's right. We're gonna have to leave. I shouldn't have told that little piss ant where we was staying. Just need to figure out where to go from here.*

Alan was leaned back on the porch swing, eyes closed, with all this running through his head when Steve joined him. He tried to hand the meth pipe to him but Steve waved it off. Leaning up against a post, he pulled a cigarette out of his pack and lit one. "I did the best I could with what I had. The bleeding has slowed down a lot. It's a mess, man. I don't know what to do with it. It's like raw meat. It's pretty gross." He paused, took a drag off the cigarette, and continued. "The vodka should help with keeping it from getting infected, but we're gonna have to watch it, and probably clean it every day. Did we have any antibiotics in the drugs we've collected? He should probably take some if we do."

"Is he gonna make it? I ain't wastin' valuable meds on him we might need down the road if he's gonna die anyway."

"I have no idea, Al. I'm not a doctor. What are you saying? You'd let him die, rather than give him some of the penicillin we've got stashed? Why did you want me to fix him up then? Why did we even bring him back?" Steve was mad and was not trying to hide it, even though he knew incurring Alan's wrath could be life-threatening itself.

"I don't know, dammit! Just get him in traveling condition for now. We're out of here in two days. We're gonna backtrack to that last place we stayed at before this one, but we need to make a stop first."

Steve eyed him suspiciously. "Two days? You want to take the chance the sheriff doesn't show up in the next two days? Where are we going then, if we aren't under arrest that is? You're not thinking of going back to that Warren place, are you? You can't take that place, Al. *We* can't take it. You're just gonna get—"

"No, not the Warren place. We're going back to the one we met those dumbasses at; what'd he say their name was? Dotson, that was it. We're going to that one."

"Why? There wasn't anything there. We checked the place good."

"No, but it's close enough to that farm that we can … never mind. Just get him ready to go." Alan got up and headed for his truck, with Steve watching and quite possibly wondering what he was going to get them in the middle of next—and if it would get them killed.

****

Two days later, with his truck crammed full of their ransacked supplies, Alan drove up the driveway to the Dotson home, having cut the lock the last time they were there when they had run into the Glass brothers. The crew had brought everything they had gathered so far with them, since there was no going back to the Callen place. Steve was still trying to get Alan to tell him why he wanted to come back here.

"This seems like a waste of time, Al. We know there's nothing here we can use. We should go on back to one of the other places we've stayed that were farther away from here. I'm telling you, the sheriff is going to be looking for us. Hell, we should get out of this county."

Alan glared at Steve. "Stop naggin' me! It's like havin' a damn wife with you around. You're riding in *my* truck. If you don't like the road I'm on, you're welcome to hit the pavement and try to make it on your own. I've got my reasons and I don't owe you shit for an explanation. Now, either get out or shut up!"

Steve set his mouth to a grim line but held his tongue. He was in a delicate position at the moment and needed to find a way out. The problem was, the longer he hung around the deeper he got involved. *I gotta get out of here,* Steve thought to himself. *Al has totally lost it and is gonna get us all killed. Problem is, I need a ride.* He had been trying to keep his eyes open for an older vehicle but so far hadn't found anything that would run. He decided to try harder to find transportation.

Rich was leaned against the passenger side door, moaning softly. Al finally relented and gave Rich some of the antibiotics he had in his stash. Steve checked and redressed the wound twice a day and had reported to Al that morning that it appeared to be healing. At least the redness was fading and it didn't smell. Both good signs as far as he could tell, not that he really knew that much about it. He had an uncle who lost an arm below the elbow in a factory accident when Steve was young. It had just been his hand that was injured. He remembered his uncle trying desperately to save his hand, against the doctor's advice; remembered it turning violent shades of red and purple, then black. But most of all he remembered the smell. They say that smells can trigger memories you can't recall otherwise. That smell was the smell of death. In the end, the gangrenous hand infected the lower section of his arm as well. He got a nice settlement from the factory, which he proceeded to drink himself to death on. He never got over the sight of his lost arm. Steve never forgot that stench. He wasn't getting any kind of smell at all from Rich's wound.

Alan drove slowly up the drive, seemingly watching for any signs of other folks there. It looked quiet, like no one had been back there. He pulled up just short of the house and got out of the truck. Steve slid out on the driver's side. Rich stayed in the cab. Alan walked around to the back of the truck and pulled two gas cans out. Steve stared at him. Knowing it would probably piss Al off again but not really caring, he started in on him again.

"What the hell are you doing with that gas? Are you fixin' to waste gas burning something? You know whatever gas is out there is it, right? Ain't no more tankers making deliveries, and no way to get it out of the ground if they did. Seriously, man—what's the deal?"

"It's my gas and I'll do whatever the hell I want to with it. Get the fuck out of my way." Alan shoved Steve aside and headed for the house. He set one of the cans down and unscrewed the lid on the one he still held. He started splashing the gas along the sides of the house working his way around it. When he had emptied the first one, he picked up the second and headed for the door going into the house. Steve stood watching him, shaking his head and mumbling "crazy, psycho sonofabitch" over and over. He walked over to the door Rich was leaning against. He knocked on the window to get Rich's attention. Rich slowly lowered the window.

"Man, what is he doin'? Why are we here? We need to get out of this place, out of this town, out of this county. I can't believe the sheriff hasn't already found us. Hey, you got any more of that Vicodin? I'm hurtin' bad, Steve."

Steve went into one of the plastic footlockers in the back of the truck and pulled out a bag of pill bottles. He shuffled through them until he found the one he needed and gave one to Rich. He put the bottle in his shirt pocket for later, placed the bag back in the bin and closed it. Rich took the pill and swallowed it dry. He closed his eyes and leaned back against the open window. Steve stood by the door looking toward the house, still shaking his head.

"I have no idea what he's doing. We should be getting the hell outta Dodge, ya know? We should just take the truck and leave his crazy ass here. Yeah, we should do that. Just go. We could be five miles away before he comes out of the house. Let's go, man. Let's do it—take his truck and go. We can—"

"No, we can't. We can't do shit. He took the keys." Rich pointed to the empty ignition on the steering column.

"Son of a bitch! He must have thought we might try to do exactly what I wanted to do. He may be a psycho, but he ain't stupid. Listen, I've been looking and haven't found anything yet so keep your eyes peeled for another old car or truck that might still be running. I want to get away from Al before he gets me killed. I'll take you with me, if you want to go that is. He's delusional, dude. He still thinks we can get in that place across the way. I'm telling ya, he's crazy and somebody over there is gonna take him out. I don't want to be around when that goes down. You with me or not?"

"Yeah, man, I'm in," Rich said, while nodding in agreement. He winced at the pain the movement caused his wound. "Al is out there, he's gone bye-bye. He's completely lost it. I don't want to be around when that shit goes down either. I ain't seen anything we could use for a ride but I ain't really been looking. I will from now on. With me by the door, I'll be able to keep an eye out without Al knowing what I'm doing. But what will we do for supplies? What will we eat? Or drink? Where will we stay?"

Steve looked toward the house, watching Alan's return. "I don't know, but I'd rather take my chances out there with nothing than here with him. At least on our own we have a chance to survive. With Al, we're dead men who just ain't died yet."

****

Alan proceeded to saturate each room in gasoline. None was spared. He wanted to make sure this fire was seen. As he made his way back to the front door, he pulled a lighter out of his pocket. He picked up a framed picture of the Dotson family from a side table in the foyer. After smashing it against the table, he pulled the photo out and lit it with his lighter. He laughed at the irony of setting the house on fire with a picture of the family who owned it. He tossed the burning image to the floor and backed out so he could watch the show. *Now, to wait for the volunteer fire department to show up*, he thought to himself. *Let's see how many fish we catch with this fire net.*

He finally turned and sauntered back to the truck where Rich and Steve were both watching him incredulously. He became defensive. "What? You never seen a house burn before? What's your problem?"

Steve shook his head. "No problem, Al, it's cool. So, what now? We gonna stay around here, see who shows up? Was that the plan all along? To try to lure them out of their place?"

Alan walked up to Steve, almost nose to nose. "What if it was? Don't you think Rich there deserves some payback for his lost ear? Forget that. Can you imagine the supplies they have in there? Those guys we had the run-in with looked pretty clean, which means they got a water source in there. What about women? You know all those fellas ain't in there without some companionship. That place is a gold mine, I can feel it. We could stay there, wait this thing out. We take that place over and we won't have to worry about nothin' else. Food, water, women—it's the perfect place, I'm tellin' ya!"

Alan had a wild look in his eye as he was relaying his fantasy of getting control of the farm and all its imagined assets. Steve looked at him incredulously. "Riiiight. So, do you think all of them will come over here to see about the fire, then? Because if they don't, we're right back where we were before. Too many of them, not enough of us."

"This is a recon mission here, dude. You are gonna stay here and hide out in that tree line over there. Me and Rich are gonna take the truck back over to that place next door to them and see what we can see. And don't you worry about there not being enough of us. This new world is gonna be ruled by guys like us. We ain't the only ones taking what we want to survive. We gotta go find some tough guys— not like those whiny bitches we found here the other day. Real bad asses, like us. Well, like me anyway." Alan laughed loudly at his dig at his companions. They didn't. "Now, get over there in them bushes. Make like a bunny rabbit—high tail it and hide. We'll come back for ya later."

Alan went around to the driver's door and climbed in. He looked over at Rich, who was leaning against the window, emitting soft moans. Alan shook his head. "Pitiful. Plumb pitiful. I oughta just shove ya out and leave ya here, let them fellas find ya when they come to check out the fire. It's not like you lost an arm or a leg. It was an ear. One lousy ear. And it's been days now. I'm tired of hearing your moanin' and groanin'. Man up and shut up!" He slammed the truck door, started it up, and pulled out of the driveway.

Chapter 2

We'd lost people. We'd lost family. We had to go on; but how did we move forward from here?

We knew there were bad people outside the "walls" of the farm but we hadn't had to come face to face with them, not really. Sure, we had encountered scavengers hell bent on taking whatever they wanted no matter who it might have belonged to or, for that matter, might still belong to. We had suffered injuries as a result. But even a gunshot wound is not the same thing as the death of one of our own. A gunshot wound will heal. The hole will eventually close, leaving behind a scar in its place. The scarred area will actually be tougher than the original skin. This wound—this loss—was going to take a whole lot longer to heal and the empty space in our hearts would probably never close. You try to move on and not wallow in the grief and sadness but that's a really hard thing to do. Life continues, despite your pain, and you still have to eat, sleep, work, and live. If you have people depending on you, your family, and friends who have become family, you can't stop living. It just feels more like existing at the time.

Life on the farm changed after the loss of Pete and Bill. Before the attack, we had been performing our assigned tasks, standing our watches, living life in the new powerless world; trying to build a lifestyle that didn't depend on electricity anymore, since there was no light at the end of the tunnel—literally. But we hadn't felt the impact of the horrors a world like this breeds until then. We still had to do those things. We just saw everything in a new, darker, more sinister view. We still had chores to do; we had livestock counting on us for food and shelter. We had vegetables growing in gardens that needed tending daily now that summer was finally here. We had a pretty large group of people who had to be fed, clothed, and protected. It was the mood and the atmosphere around us that had changed. We were no longer untouched by the evil that was lurking outside our home. We had experienced firsthand what the world was becoming— an ugly and dangerous place.

Where before we had the feeling of safety in being invisible to the world, now we felt exposed. Steps were taken to reinforce what were perceived as weak points. The opening Pete had cleared was covered over with deadfall and made to look impassible, which it pretty much was. We couldn't put the trees back that had been pulled up or pushed over, but we piled them up as a natural barrier that no one was going to drive over or through. A lookout post was set up in the barn loft which could oversee the house, the bunk-house, the small livestock pens, and the campground. Sheets of metal roofing had been hoisted up to create a protection barrier with a row of sandbags on either side of it. The same was done at the tree house. We were no longer hidden from the outside world so we tried to prepare for the next fight, which everyone was sure was coming.

Sara was mourning the loss of her husband but she still had Tony to take care of and appeared to be pushing her grief down as she worked to protect her son. Her entire outlook on the world around her changed. No longer was she worried about other people's children. She was focused on her own. She seemed to become obsessed with his safety and consequently his ability to keep himself and everyone around him safe. They both went to gun training class every time it was held, which was every day again. We needed everyone to be armed at all times and we needed them to know how to handle a pistol or revolver, to be proficient with their sidearm of choice, as well as at least one rifle, and to always be on guard for any situation that might call upon them to use it. We had emergency drills where Mike and Monroe taught us how to react to different situations, including tactical movements that involved every man or woman over the age of fifteen. It scared the hell out of me to see my son doing drills used by our military, and I hoped and prayed he'd never have to use that knowledge. Everyone also learned how to clean pretty much any gun on the place because a clean gun is a more reliable gun as everyone knows. Even the smaller kids were taught how to use a boresnake and could load magazines with the help of a tool called an Uplula. Sara brought Tony with her to every training. She wanted him to be able to protect and defend himself if she wasn't with him, which wasn't very often these days. He had no qualms about learning to use a gun and they both turned out to be pretty decent shots. Tony could be found sitting on the front porch or patrolling the yard with a rifle when he wasn't doing chores. While he was still too young for security watches, he took it upon himself to become the house patrol. Sara and Tony had taken their tragedy and heartache and used it as the reason to change the course of their lives. They appeared to be coming out of this stronger and more self-reliant than before. Pete would have been proud.

Ryan went through a much larger change, actually the biggest transformation of us all. He was a completely different person. Gone was the fun-loving, always laughing and cracking jokes young man we had come to know and love. Left in his place was a quiet, sullen, empty soul. He took every security shift Mike would let him have and spent that time in the tree house with binoculars trained as far as he could see. If anyone had asked me, I would have said he was constantly looking for the men who killed his brother. Would he know them if he saw them out there? Did he get a good enough look at them? That was a question I had asked him when we served a watch together.

"Yes, Anne, I'd know them. I picked a random one out of the bunch and took him out but I saw the rest of them through the rifle scope. I'll never forget their faces and I won't rest until I know every one of those murdering bastards is dead."

I knew he had every right to feel the way he did but the loss of our lovable Ryan was so hard to handle. I was afraid his obsession would take him down a darker path than even the killers were on. Would he ever know joy again?

"Oh honey, I know you're hurting. But it won't always be like this. The pain won't always be so raw. You'll find a place to store it inside you so that you can go on and find happiness, maybe even find someone to be happy and share your life with. Bill wouldn't want you to stop living because he's gone. I'm sure he would want you to live life to the fullest for his sake, in his honor. Do you think he would want you harboring all this hatred because of him?"

Ryan turned to me with complete calm. "He'd do it for me, make sure they paid. Besides, I'm not that goofy little brother anymore. I've changed on the inside. It's like when you break a car window. It shatters into hundreds of pieces. It will never be the same again. Even if you try to put it back together—even if you could—it would never be like it was. It would become something new, something different. That's how I feel, Anne. I've picked up the pieces, and tried to put them back together, but I'm not the same. I don't think I'll ever again be the 'me' I was before Bill was killed. The new me is broken and mended … but definitely something else."

I fought the urge to wrap my arms around him and hold him until he released it all but I knew that wasn't what he wanted or needed. He wanted distance from relationships of all kinds and needed his space to work things out. I turned away and wiped the tears from my face as I headed for the ladder off the Bird's Nest. None of us could help him with this because he wouldn't let us. We just had to be patient and wait for him to come back to us.

Dear God, please bring him back to us.

****

As the male and female animals had been brought together for breeding to increase meat production, there was a lot of activity on the farm that the younger "city" kids had never seen before. The Scanlin girls and the Roush kids watched wide-eyed one morning as the bull, Titan, started the day off with his own chore—making more cows. There were a few heifers in season so he was availing himself of his harem. Moira and Aiden ran to their dad screaming, "Dad! Dad! That big cow is attacking the other cows! We need to stop him! He's hurting them!"

Matt and Nick had been standing by the fence watching the interactions of the livestock, followed by the former city kids' reactions to it, and were laughing at the younger ones' angst. Bob walked up behind them and gave them both a smack on the back of the head at the same time. They winced, rubbing their noggins. Matt whined, "Dang, that hurt, Mr. Bob. What'd you do that for?"

Bob had crossed his arms over his chest and was scowling at them. "For making fun of those kids. Do you think if you were their age and had grown up in the city you'd know what was going on out there? You need to be setting an example. You're damn near grown. They need to know how to live in this world. Teach them. No, you don't need to tell them about the birds and the bees, but you could at least let them know that Titan ain't hurtin' them cows. Then their parents can explain the, er, specifics to them."

They both looked down, embarrassment on their faces. Nick spoke for them. "Sorry. We ain't had a lot to laugh about lately and I guess we picked the wrong time. We'll talk to them."

Bob looked over and saw Lee and Kate talking to all four kids. "It's alright. Looks like their parents are working on that right now. Y'all get on with your chores. I'm sure you've got something you're supposed to be working on."

"Yes sir," both boys replied as they headed for the barn. Monroe was coming out and saw the chastised looks on their faces as they passed him. He walked over to Bob by the fence.

"What's up with them boys? You catch 'em smokin' behind the barn or somethin'?"

Bob relayed the story to his uncle, who snickered quietly. "Yeah, I reckon that's somethin' city kids ain't ever seen before. Thought ole Titan was attacking them cows and heifers, huh?"

Bob grinned. "Yeah, and it is kind of funny. They'll laugh about it themselves in a few years, I'm sure. Kind of makes you wonder what city folks are thinking about this new way of life, how they're getting by."

Monroe snorted. "You think there's a bunch of 'em still alive, do ya? My guess is unless they were real smart and figured out what was going on, and that they were in the worst spot they could be, there ain't many city people still alive—not any decent ones anyway. They'd have been trying to 'get through it' and 'hold out for the government to show up to help' and most likely killed for whatever they did or didn't have by gangs. Nah, I'd bet the good folks are dead and gone. Only ones left in the cities are the parasites and assholes."

Bob nodded solemnly. "You know, I'd like to think that I was smart enough to know when this happened that we needed to get out here, but if it weren't for Russ and Anne turning us into preppers we wouldn't have had a vehicle that would have made it through the pulse to drive here. If we'd had to try to walk here, we wouldn't have had the supplies we did after we went down this path, and most likely wouldn't have made it. I wouldn't have known all the things I know now about surviving. I didn't think I needed to know. I can't imagine how everything would be now if we hadn't prepared for something like this."

"Yep, I've thought about that, too. Millie and I would have been alright, I think, but we wouldn't have had so much stored up, especially stuff like gas and kerosene, solar panels, that kind of thing. And I never would have even thought about camouflaging the front. Hell, that's part of living in the country; you and your neighbors are there for each other. But then, it ain't the neighbors we've got to worry about now, is it?"

Bob shook his head. "Nope. I'm afraid we may be dealing with those city gangs in the not too distant future, too. Where else are they gonna go? The food in the cities has got to be running low, or out. They'll head for the country, hoping to find places like ours. It'll get ugly, fast."

Monroe turned toward the house. "I don't reckon there's much we can do about that, son. All we can do is keep living life the best we can for now. If it happens, we'll deal with it then. No sense in worrying about somethin' that ain't happened yet."

Bob followed his uncle across the yard. "No sir, there isn't, but I'm betting we'll be dealing with something before the summer is out. I've just got a feeling …"

As they approached the porch, they overheard Kate offering a G-rated explanation of the behavior of the livestock.

"You may see the boy and girl animals close together, and it may look like one of them is hurting the other, but it is perfectly natural. That is how babies are made. We need them to make more of their kind so we have food to eat this winter. Do you understand?"

The kids had seen deer, rabbits, wild turkeys, even a wild boar, cleaned and cut up. Their shock at finding out where their food came from was quickly overcome by a child's innate curiosity about pretty much everything. They took part in the butchering along with everyone else. They were much less affected by how the meat came to be on the table than by how the meat got started in the first place.

Katlyn was looking up at her mother. "But, we don't eat the babies, right, Mommy?"

Kate smiled. "No, honey, we wait for them to grow up first."

Katlyn shrugged her shoulders. "Okay, Mommy. We need to go do our chores now." She skipped off, her sister and a couple of dogs following.

Kate laughed and turned to Lee. "Well, I think mine are good. How about yours?"

Lee was watching his kids for any signs of confusion or trauma. "Guys? Do you understand, too? That it's how nature works and how we grow more food?"

Aiden was nodding but Moira was still wide-eyed. That was probably a lot of info for a six-year-old to take in. She slowly nodded as well.

"Yeah, it's cool, Dad. I get it now." He glanced at his little sister. Wrapping an arm around her shoulders, he led her toward the rabbit hutches. "C'mon sis. Let's go pet the bunnies." He turned around and mouthed to his dad, "She'll be okay," and gave his dad a thumbs-up. Lee grinned at him and returned the gesture. He looked back at Kate.

"They are resilient, aren't they? To think, a few months ago I was trying to decide whether or not to sign Aiden up for t-ball and Moira for ballet. Now, I'm worrying about whether or not they are traumatized about how babies are made. I think it bothered me more than them."

Kate nodded. "If only everything in this new world could be explained and dealt with so easily."

Lee watched his kids walk across the yard with a far-off look in his eye. "If only."

****

Mike and Russ had the electronics for the solar panels spread out in the back of the barn. There were a couple of pallets of golf cart batteries there, along with a pallet of deep-cycle marine batteries. Mike was surveying the equipment, which included the solar panels and rolls of large electrical wire.

"I'd say we can have a nice amount of power with all this. I'll admit, though, I've never seen a setup with the smaller golf cart batteries. They're only half the voltage; seems it would take a lot more of them to achieve the voltage you're after, twice as many."

Russ looked at the pallets and then to Mike. "It does, but by using both the six-volt batteries and the twelve-volt we can have a longer running system."

"How so?" Mike asked.

"Well think about it. A car, or boat in this case, needs a large amount of juice to get started. Then, once it's started, it will slowly recharge the battery while the vehicle is running. They keep things going, but the biggest draw on the battery is on startup. A golf cart, on the other hand, doesn't have a big energy draw on start up. It's a pretty constant usage level, thus a constant drain as it runs down. So, by using both types together, we get the best of both worlds. Plus, the golf cart batteries are actually cheaper in the long run, take up less space, and are a good bit lighter."

Mike looked puzzled. "So, you're going to hook them all up together? How does that work?"

"The batteries are hooked up both in series and parallel. Parallel is positive to positive and negative to negative. Series is positive to negative. When we connect two twelve-volt batteries parallel, we end up with a battery that has twice the power but is still twelve volts. The series set up with the same two batteries produces a twenty-four-volt battery with the same current as one. You follow?"

Mike was nodding now. "Yeah, I'm with you so far. Which one are you going to use?"

Russ grinned. "Both."

"Huh?"

"Yeah, we wire them with both set ups to produce higher voltage and current. You can put as many together as you want. The batteries don't care."

"Man, you really were ready for this, huh?"

"I tried to be as ready as I could be for whatever happened. Honestly, this was the scenario I considered the least likely. I'm just glad I read up on stuff like this, just in case. But even if it had been any other apocalyptic event, sooner or later the power would go down. Those systems don't stay running without maintenance. Did you even think twice about your job when everything went to shit? I didn't, Anne didn't, and Bob was on his way to work when it happened. Turned around immediately and came home."

Mike shook his head. "No, I was thinking about how much food I didn't have. I was one of those people, the ones who didn't keep much food in the house. Single guy, never really into cooking, it was just as easy to throw a TV dinner in the microwave or pick something up on the way home. I did have a nice stock of Vienna sausages and crackers though. Don't know why, but I love those nasty little wieners. Try making a case of those and a couple of boxes of crackers last more than a week. Not happening. Fortunately, I did know how to hunt, though I hadn't done it for years. I did realize it wasn't just a power outage pretty quick. That helped me start planning."

"Fortunately for all of us, we've been planning for years. I hate that it happened, but I'm glad we were ready. Well, as ready as we could be."

"So am I, buddy, and very glad we met. I can't imagine where I'd be right now if it weren't for this place, or the folks we had with us then. Especially the ones with kids."

Russ smiled at him. "Everything happens for a reason. There was a reason Brian and I found the Scanlins the first time, there was a reason they found you, and there was a reason we all found each other. This was supposed to happen. Now, what do you say we try to get some power up in here?"

Mike was unwinding the heavy electrical wire. "Let's do it."

Chapter 3

The trial of Clay Glass never happened.

The scene at the Glass home was nothing short of macabre. Rhonda had walked out of the front door of their trailer when she heard the trucks pull up. Seeing her son's body lying in the bed of Clay's truck, she rushed over to it and fell on Jay's body keening and wailing, "My boy! My baby boy! Lord, they've killed my little boy!" It was apparent she truly loved her sons. The pain emanating from her was genuine and so strong the men could feel it, like a physical wave of heat against their faces. Clay went to his mother and tried to pull her to him but she jerked away and laid her head back on her younger son's lifeless form. Gary waited for her sobs to subside. When she seemed to be getting control of herself, he spoke quietly to her.

"Ms. Glass, I am so sorry for your loss. I know you're hurting right now, but—"

She jerked herself up and pierced him with a hate-filled glare. "*Yes*! I *am* hurting! I'm dying inside right now! Who did this? Did you arrest them, Sheriff? I want to know who murdered my son!"

Gary took a step back from the verbal assault, knowing the woman was grieving. He reached out to lay a hand on her shoulder, to comfort her.

"No, ma'am, we didn't arrest anybody. There's more to this story than you know. You see …"

She jerked away from him. "*No*, I do *not* see! What is there to see? My son was butchered! Someone has to be held accountable for this crime!"

Tim stepped between her and Gary, his frustration with the woman's emotions and abuse rushing forth—from his mouth. "Lady, your *baby boy* was part of the ambush and murder of two innocent men. You need to back off."

Gary looked at him with a mix of gratitude and exasperation. Gratitude for the support; exasperation for exacerbating the situation with his bluntness.

Rhonda stood with her mouth hanging open. "You lie! That's a bald-faced lie! My sons would never do anything like that. Clay, tell him he's wrong."

She turned to the one son she had left, no doubt expecting him to vindicate his brother and himself. Clay stood with his head bowed, not looking at his mother, or anyone for that matter. He spoke just above a whisper.

"It's true, Momma. We was there," he replied, but then quickly added, "but we didn't shoot nobody. We didn't even want to be involved. They made us. They threatened to kill us, then come find you and kill you, too—after they beat and raped you. We had to go, Momma! We didn't want to, but we had to! Forgive me, Momma! Please forgive me!"

Clay fell to his knees at his mother's feet, sobbing. Rhonda looked down at him with fresh tears flowing and caressed his head. "Oh, honey, it's not your fault. You was just tryin' to provide for us, now wasn't ya? Tryin' to take care of your momma and protect her, and just got tangled up with the wrong folks. Can't nobody fault you for that."

"Actually, we can, Ms. Glass. He is guilty by association, because he was with those guys when they shot and killed two men from the Warren place. I'm afraid I'm going to have to take him in as soon as we get your other son buried. We brought him here as a courtesy to you, out of respect for your loss. Once we get Jay laid to rest, we're heading to the office and he's coming with us." Gary was compassionate but firm.

"*No*! I'm not losing both of my boys on the same day! You can't do this to me, Sheriff! I need him to help me; I'm disabled, you know. I can't get around very well, and we're about out of food. My boys have been scavenging the empty houses in the area since everything went off. They ain't hurt anyone, ain't taken from no one, 'cept what folks was willing to give. I can't make it without him; I'll die without him! He's all I have left!" Rhonda started wailing again. Tim looked heavenward. Gary shook his head and looked down as he dug a hole in the dirt with the toe of his boot.

"I'm sorry, ma'am, but he has to come with us. We need him to tell us what led up to them gunning down two people who were doing nothing more than getting along in this new world and who were actually trying to help us get set up to plant some good-sized crops to feed the people here in town. Scavenging is fine as long as there's something to scavenge. What happens when all that food is gone? It won't be long until that's the case, if we aren't already there. What will people do then? Winter will be here before we know it and if we don't have some food stores built up and put back, a lot of folks are going to starve, including you. I'm pretty sure this chain of events has screwed that whole plan and now we are going to have to find some way to either fix it or come up with a new one. Every day that goes by that we don't have crops in the ground is another growing day wasted. We don't have time for this shit!" Gary was getting worked up now. The wailing was grating on his nerves. "Now tell me where you want your boy buried so we can be done with that and get back to figuring out how to feed a thousand people this winter!"

Rhonda was indignant. "How dare you talk to me like that! I'm the victim here! I'm—"

"You're shutting up now," Tim replied quietly, with a veiled threat. "The sheriff has spent enough time trying to make you understand. This is not just about you, *Rhonda*. It's about the whole

29

damn town. Now, either tell us where to bury Jay or we can just go on with our business and leave him like this for you to deal with. Alone."

She opened her mouth to say something else, then closed it. With her lips set to a thin line, she turned and walked to the back side of her trailer where a small garden from a previous tenant had been laid out many years before. She pointed to the spot, taking on a whiny tone. "Here. Bury him here where he'll be close and I can come talk to him while I'm alone and starving to death. Then you won't have far to carry my body to lay beside him when you find me dead one day, wasted away to nothin'."

Clay rushed to his mother's side. "You ain't dyin', Momma! I'll be back as quick as I can. I'm gonna help the sheriff find those assholes so he can bring them to justice. I'll get immunity for doing that, right Sheriff Burns?"

Gary looked at Tim, who shrugged and said, "It would solve the problem of what to do with him, since we can't feed him. He wouldn't be given the death penalty for being there, Sheriff. He'd probably get prison time though."

Gary looked thoughtful. "Hmm. Maybe we could make his garden work time mandatory, like the old working prisons used to be. He could stay here with his mother at night, but during the day he works full time in the community garden—that is if there still *is* a community garden."

Clay was nodding his head vigorously. "I could do that, Sheriff. I surely could. Then I can still look after my momma here."

Rhonda was grinning until she saw Gary watching her. She toned it down to a small smile. "Thank you, Sheriff Burns. I'll feel much better having my only son with me, at least at night. Would you say a few words over Jay's grave, since we ain't got a preacher close by?"

"Uh, well, I guess I could, um, do that. Sure." Gary looked uncomfortable, and Tim was snickering at him. Gary glared at Tim. "Something funny, Deputy? This isn't a laughing matter. Go get the shovel and get to digging. We need to get back to the office."

Tim stopped laughing. He had a look of indignation on his face as he grabbed a shovel out of the back of Gary's truck and headed around the trailer. On the way, he spied another one lying on the ground, rusted from the weather. He picked it up, carried it with him and handed it to Clay. "Here. Might as well get used to handling things like shovels and hoes. You're going to be spending a lot of time with them. Get to digging."

"Sure thing, Deputy. No problem." Clay took the shovel with a satisfied look on his face. What was he up to now?

****

By the time they got to the jail, Clay had filled the sheriff in on everything he knew about Alan and his crew, including his thoughts about where they were holed up. Tim never said a word about knowing the guys. Gary questioned him further. "What makes you think they're at the Callen place, Clay? Did they tell you that?"

"Yeah, Sheriff, they said they was staying out there, that the Callens were friends of theirs. That Alan guy said the Callens must have been gone when it all went down, cuz they hadn't been home. Do you think those guys might have killed them?"

Gary shook his head. "No, thank God. Luke and Casey Callen are at the Warren farm. They did have a run-in with those men before they left their home, and again as they were leaving to go stay with the Warren group. My guess is they knew the Callens had left because they saw them pulling out with their camper. They just didn't know where they went."

"Well, I bet if you go out there, you'll find them. They did the shootin', Sheriff. Me and Jay didn't even raise our guns. We didn't want to go, but he made us, Alan that is. We ain't hurt nobody, and Jay got killed anyway! You gotta believe me, Sheriff Burns— this wasn't our idea. We just go to houses that are empty and see if they have food; you know, like the folks didn't get back after everything went off. We ain't done harm to a livin' soul."

"So you keep saying, Clay. You're innocent, you were just minding your own business and these guys showed up at the

Dotson home at the same time as you and shanghaied you and your brother into showing them how to get into the Warren farm. Now, explain this to me: I know for a fact that you had been to the Dotson place before. Jim told me he ran you off when you tried to climb in his kitchen window after they wouldn't give you any more handouts. If you were only going to houses that you knew for sure no one was there, what were you doing back at their place? You didn't know they were gone. Were you looking for trouble with Jim again, because that's what it sounds like to me."

Clay went wide-eyed. "N-no, Sheriff, we wasn't lookin' for no trouble. Pickins' is gettin' slim now from the empty houses. We thought they were still there. I was gonna beg old man—er, Mr. Dotson to let us work on his place for some more food and stuff. They had a pretty decent sized garden and with no equipment to work it, we figured he'd be needin' some farm hands." Gary knew Clay was lying through his teeth, probably hoping the sheriff couldn't tell. Wishful thinking.

"Don't give me that bullshit, Clay. You haven't worked a minute for anything you've gotten up until now, outside of breaking into people's homes. I guess you consider jimmying doors and busting windows work. I thought a couple of times you were gonna pass out digging your brother's grave and it isn't even that hot out yet. I doubt Jim would have traded you much food for a whole ten minutes of work."

33

Tim snorted with laughter. Clay's face turned red and he looked like he was about to cuss Tim and Gary both but he held his tongue. Instead he replied, "I know I've been kind of a slacker, but I'm turning over a new leaf, Sheriff. I want to help my town. I've seen what happens when you get tangled up with the wrong people, even though we wasn't tryin' to. You tell me what you need me to do and I'm there. Scout's honor."

Tim looked at him with a smirk. "Like you were ever a Boy Scout."

Clay apparently couldn't stand the smart-mouthed deputy one second longer. "Yeah, I don't reckon either one of us was good enough to go down that road, huh Tim?"

Tim started toward Clay but Gary put a hand across his chest. "Okay fellas, that'll do. Clay, I'm going to let you go on home to your momma. You are to go straight there and stay there until tomorrow morning. First thing in the morning I want you back here. We'll put you to cleaning up around the station until we get this crop situation worked out. First thing, not ten or noon. Understood?"

Clay was watching Tim, but nodded at Gary. "Absolutely, Sheriff. I'll be here." He smiled at Gary, flipped Tim off behind his back, and headed out the door.

****

When he got to the sheriff's office the next morning, Clay knocked on the locked door and was let in by Gary. He looked around and figured out that someone was living there. Clothes were hanging from ropes strung across one end of the room, including women's apparel. *What the hell is going on up in here? Who all is staying here?* As if in answer to his unspoken question, Mayor Angie Hale came around the corner from the break room with a water packet and a cereal bar. He peered past her into the room. When he saw all the rations in there, he was livid—inside. *Where did all that stuff come from? What right do they have to keep it for themselves?* Outside, he acted like nothing was any different. Inside, he was trying to figure out how to get his hands on some of it to take home for him and his mom. Outside, he pretended to not even know what they were. Angie stopped when she saw him. She gave Gary a questioning look.

"Oh, Angie—Mayor Hale, this is Clay Glass. I told you about him. He's the one who will be working for us in a lot of different capacities to pay his debt to society for the awful scenario he was involved in at the Warren farm, though he wasn't the shooter. Clay, this is Mayor Angie Hale."

Angie moved both food and water to her left hand, and extended her right to Clay. "Hello Clay. I'm happy to see you were open to alternate methods of sentencing for your infractions, and that hopefully you are striving to become a productive member of our community. It will take all of us working together to survive this situation, especially when winter gets here."

Clay shook her hand. "Yes, ma'am. I've got my momma to take care of, so I'm willing to do whatever I have to, to make sure she has food to eat and stays warm this winter, even though that's a long way off."

"Yes, but it will be here before we know it, and we have a lot of work to do to get ready for it. It's easy to not think about it when the temperature outside is eighty degrees or more. That will be a completely different story six or seven months from now when it could quickly drop into the twenties. Gary, I'd like to sit down with you this morning and talk about the garden situation, as well as making plans for this winter; as soon as you're done here, of course."

Gary nodded. "Let me get Clay situated and I'll be right back." Angie smiled and continued on to his office. Clay was eyeballing the MREs in the break room when Gary turned back to him. Clay caught the movement from the sheriff and focused on him instead.

"So, what you want me to work on this morning, Sheriff? Sweeping up? Maybe organizing those supplies in there? How can I help?"

Gary walked over and pulled the break room door closed. "Your first chore may be the toughest. Follow me." He led Clay back to the men's room and reached for the handle. Clay grimaced, certain he would be assaulted with a horrendous smell; one he had smelled more than once since the water stopped flowing. As the sheriff pushed the door open, Clay was surprised. While there was a slight odor, it wasn't nearly as bad as some of the ones he'd encountered over the past few weeks.

"Wow. I was expectin' that to smell real bad, but it ain't bad at all. How are you able to use the toilets still, Sheriff?"

Gary kept walking to the back stall. "We aren't exactly using a toilet per se. We have what are called honey buckets. It's basically a bucket with a toilet seat and a trash bag like liner to collect the waste. You need to take the lid off, which will increase the smell quickly, close the bag and change it out for a new one. We have one in here and one in the ladies' room. I want both of them bagged up and a new one put in. You'll find spare bags in the utility closet just outside, along with a broom and some antibacterial wipes. I want you to sweep the floors in both bathrooms, and wipe down the sinks with one of those wipes. Make sure the bucket seats are cleaned, too, but do those *after* the sinks are done in both. Try to only use one wipe, two at the most. There won't be any more of those made for a while. Take the toilet bags out back. You'll see a dumpster across the alley where we've been depositing them. Come see me when you're done."

Gary turned and walked out. Clay looked at the bucket then back at the door the sheriff had just gone through. *I bet I can milk this gig for at least an hour, maybe two. Drag this out 'til lunchtime, and see what kind of food they got in them packs in there.* Clay stood beside the bucket, smiling. *Yeah, a little shit work here and there might just get some good supplies for me and Momma. This might turn out to be a great setup.* He headed for the utility room, at a slow, easy gait. No reason to rush things.

****

Angie was sitting on the sofa in the sheriff's office when Gary came in and shut the door behind him. He went to his desk and sat on the edge, giving her his full attention. "Now, what can I do for you, Madam Mayor?" He had a teasing tone to his voice and a grin on his face. Angie, however, was all business.

"Gary, is the Warren farm still an option? After what happened …"

Gary dropped the grin, looked at her, and shook his head. "I truly don't know, Angie. After what transpired, I wouldn't be at all surprised if it went to hell, and knowing how cantankerous Monroe can be, I'd be more surprised if he said yes now, to be honest. And I can't say I'd blame him at all."

"What are we going to do about feeding the townsfolk if he backs out? Do we have any other avenues or options?"

"Not at the moment. We'll see what he says. I plan on going back out there in a couple of days. I know we don't have time to waste, but we have to give them time to grieve."

"Of course, that makes perfect sense. On another note, though related: I want to see who in town is in the worst shape and start handing out some of these food and water rations. I'm thinking we can surely give them three meals per person plus water pouches. I know that isn't much but hopefully it will help. We don't even know how many folks are still around or alive, for that matter. We need a town meeting as soon as possible. I'd like to get a thorough count of the supplies today and hand it out tomorrow. Is that doable?"

"I don't see why not. And I think three meals apiece is a good number. Then, if we have leftovers, we can knock on some doors if the folks don't get to the meeting and distribute them. But, I have to get back out to the Warren place day after tomorrow, no later. We have to know where we stand and, if they decide to rescind their offer, we have to come up with a backup plan. Fast."

Angie stood up and opened the door. She looked at Gary with conviction. "We'll do whatever we have to do, Sheriff, to take care of our town and our people. Now, let's go do inventory."

Tim was coming out of the break room with both hands full of cereal bars, instant oatmeal, and water packets. Angie put her hands on her hips and huffed disgustedly. "Excuse me, Deputy, but just what do you think you're doing?"

Tim looked at her and said simply, "Breakfast."

Gary stepped in and took all but one oatmeal pack and one water from him. "This is not an all you can eat buffet, Tim. We eat just enough to get by. Even that's going to change real soon."

"What do you mean? What's happening?" Tim's voice trembled with either anger or fright—or both.

"You'll find out tomorrow, when everyone else does. We need to get a current count on everything food and water related right now. Pick one MRE for tonight, and that's all you get today."

"One meal? How am I supposed to live on that?"

Angie brushed past him on her way into the break room. "I guess you're about to find out."

****

Clay did not get any of the food rations, aside from three meals each for himself and his mother. He was disappointed, especially when the sheriff locked the break room door after the inventory was done, but there was no way he was breaking into a room inside the sheriff's office building. *Damn it! Now I'm gonna have to figure out some other way to get Momma some food.* He was contemplating how to do that when the sheriff addressed him.

"Clay, you'll continue to clean up here, as well as pick up trash outside. I'm going to request that everyone keep the street in front of their home clean here in town, so you will be responsible for the street out front. Once we start working the gardens, and the crops start coming in, you will get a portion for yourself just like everyone else working there. Your work is mandatory, but you'll still receive food rations. It will only be for you, but you can share it with your mother. If she chooses to try to work the garden, she can get her own portion."

Clay was surprised at the sheriff's offer. "Really? I get food, even though this is my punishment? That's great, Sheriff. But, as far as my momma goes, I don't know if she'd be able to help, what with being disabled and all."

"Anybody with two hands can sit in a chair and shell peas or shuck corn. But, it's up to her. You let her know."

"I will, Sheriff. Just don't hold your breath."

Chapter 4

"Guys! Look! I see smoke! Can you smell it? Something is burning and it's big!" Brian yelled down from the tree house to Bob and Ben in the foxholes.

Bob pulled out binoculars as he was climbing out of the hole. "I can't see anything from down here. Can you tell where it's coming from?"

Brian looked through the set of binoculars we kept in the overlook. "Yeah, I think so. You better call up to the house. I think it's the Dotson place."

Bob got on the radio and hailed Millie in the kitchen. "Aunt Millie! Get Jim and Monroe! Get Russ and Mike! Hell, get everybody! It looks like Jim and Charlotte's house is on fire!"

Russ grabbed the radio in the kitchen and replied, "Shit! Are you sure? We're on our way!"

Everyone grabbed their rifles and packs, and burst through the front door in a beeline to the gate. Mike, the former Marine, was in much better shape than most, and beat everyone there. In their defense, he was already outside and heard the commotion so he had a head start. He was already up in the overlook checking the area. He called down to the rest of the group, reporting what he was seeing.

"Yep, it looks to be coming from Jim's place. Man, it looks bad. Sorry, Jim." He looked down to where Jim was standing with his daughters, trying to catch his breath along with everyone else. Charlotte was in no shape to walk out here, much less run. Ashley and Carrie started crying and hugging each other. Their dad wrapped his arms around both of his daughters.

"It's just a house. Four walls and a roof. Thank God, we weren't there. It'll be okay, girls." He tried consoling his daughters with words that might ease the pain of their loss. That house was the only home they had ever known. Every memory of their childhood was within those four walls. And even though he was trying hard to be strong for his girls, you could hear the pain and heartbreak in his voice.

Ryan calmly headed for the gate. "I'm going over there to see if whoever started it is still there." He wasn't asking anyone for their input. He was stating a fact.

Mike climbed down and hurried after him. "Hold up, buddy. I'm going, too."

At that, Russ and Bob joined their group, with Jim bringing up the rear. His daughters started after them as well, but Jim stopped them. "Girls, please stay here with your mom. I don't want her worrying about all of us. I'm sure if someone is responsible for this they are long gone but we'll take a radio. We'll let you know what we find."

Reluctantly, they complied with their father's wishes. Ashley took over Bob's spot in the foxhole. Carrie turned toward the house to go let her mom know what was going on, not something she was looking forward to. She turned back, taking them all in, then lingering slightly on Ryan. "Be careful. Don't take any chances. Call if you see anybody there. We'll bring the cavalry."

The response was a round of thumbs-up and a small smile from Ryan. Janet grabbed Bob by the arm and spoke low to him. "Why don't you guys take a truck? It is not safe out there. I've got a bad feeling about this fire. You need to be able to get away fast and you can't do that on foot."

He looked at her, then Russ, who gave a slight shake of his head. Russ replied, "Because we'd have to 'unlock' the gate to get a truck out, which would mean moving the center post and leaving it out until we came back. I'm worried about the cause of this fire myself. What if it's meant to be a distraction to get us to open the gate? A bunch of us leave to go check it out and now our manpower defenses are reduced as well as leaving the front door open. We can get over there in about twenty minutes at a jog, maybe less. Keep an eye on things here. Put everyone on alert until we find out what happened."

She nodded grimly and hugged her husband fiercely. "Be safe. Come back to me."

Bob hugged her back, dropped a kiss on her forehead, and grinned as he let go. "Always." He headed for the gate where the rest of the group were already climbing over. Janet stood there chewing on a cuticle watching them walk away.

****

I hugged Russ and blew him a kiss, which he caught, then waved as they made their way off the farm. I walked up and linked my arm in Janet's. "C'mon, sister. Let's get everybody in their designated places for Defcon 2."

She looked at me with worry and fear. "Are we ever going to be able to relax and just live a decent life, Anne? Or is it always going to be one issue, one emergency, one catastrophe after another? It's barely been a few days since we buried Pete and Bill. I can't handle any more pain, loss, or death right now."

I pulled my arm from hers and wrapped her in a hug. "I don't know, honey. I honestly don't know if this is what our lives will be from here on out, or just for the next few months, or even the foreseeable future. Nothing in the world out there is getting better. More and more people are running out of food and water. They are becoming desperate to feed themselves and their families. There will be lots of people on the roads trying to find something, anything to eat. If they've lasted this long, they either had supplies or are really good at finding them. However, there's only so much prepared food out there. There are no more deliveries. From now until whenever everything gets fixed and functioning again, food will come from the source: the plant, the animal, whatever the case may be. Unfortunately, there are so many people—most of them, in fact—who know absolutely nothing about how to grow those things. We will have to stay vigilant at all times. If a large group of people outside of this place knew we were here and what we have, we'd be overrun and most likely lose a lot more of our family. I wish I had something more positive to say but this is what we do now to take care of us."

Janet wiped her eyes with the tail of her shirt. "Yeah, I figured as much. I guess I just needed to hear it out loud. It really sucks, you know?"

We started walking toward the house. I kept an arm around her shoulders. "It does, indeed, suck."

****

Mike led the way at a brisk walk, stopping every fifty yards or so to listen for any sound that didn't belong. The closer they got to the Dotson farm, the stronger the smell of smoke was in the air. The wind was blowing against their backs, so they weren't getting the full effect of the smoke cloud. As they got to the edge of the property, they could see the house engulfed in flames. There was no saving it, not that they had a chance to with no running water.

There was a well on the place, but of course the pump was electric and since the Dotsons weren't really preppers, they hadn't considered having an alternative way to get water out of the ground. Alert to anything out of the ordinary, besides the house burning down in front of them, they skirted around the inferno checking the area. The heat from the flames had them cutting a wide path around the house. They were looking for whatever might have started the fire, and Jim found it.

"Guys, over here." The group hurried to where Jim was standing. At his feet were two five-gallon gas cans, lying empty on their sides.

"I was thinkin' the whole way over here it had to be deliberate. I flipped the main breaker off when we left, just in case the power came back on, not that I expected it to. Shut off the gas line, too. No way the place caught fire with no one here. Someone set this fire, wasting precious gasoline in doing it, I might add. But why? What would they have to gain from it?" Jim looked confused and angry as he gave one of the empty cans a kick that sent it skittering several feet away.

"Who would do this? It had to be just for sheer meanness." Bob was angry as he said it and this wasn't even his home. But when you've worked hard your entire adult life for everything you have, you can understand and imagine how you would feel if it were your property that had been destroyed, apparently out of spite. Everyone tried not to think about what kind of shape the homes they had abandoned were in, or if they were even still standing. No one talked about it much because it just led to a bunch of what-ifs there was no time for now.

"I was talking about this right before we left," Russ said. "It could be this was set to try to get us to open the gate and drive over to investigate it. With the gate open waiting for our return, and us gone, the farm would be more vulnerable. I don't know if that's the reason but it's a good theory, in my opinion."

Ryan immediately brought his rifle to his shoulder to scan the area through the scope. "You think they're watching us now?"

All the men went on alert and quickly followed Ryan's example. After a thorough scan in all directions, none of them saw anyone else in the area so they relaxed just a bit after a minute or so. "I don't see anyone, but let's keep our eyes and ears peeled, gang," Mike commented as he continued to survey the surrounding landscape.

"Seems like your idea is a pretty sound one, Russ," Mike replied. "My money is on those assholes that killed Pete and Bill." He looked over at Ryan, who turned to them at the mention of his brother's name.

"I hope it is them. I hope they're close, watching us right now," Ryan said with a deadly calm, then went back to scanning the area through the scope of his rifle. "I'd just as soon finish this now as later. They're going to pay for murdering my brother. That's a given. The only unknown now is when."

Mike acknowledged the comments with a curt nod. "Yes, they will, buddy. And when the time comes, we will handle it, together. Agreed?"

Ryan turned to Mike, seemed to consider what he had said, then gave him a nod in return. "I'd like that. My only condition is I get to take out the leader. Cool?"

Mike glanced over Ryan's shoulder to where the rest of the guys were watching the interaction with concerned looks on their faces. He refocused on Ryan. "Okay, Ryan. He's yours."

Ryan almost smiled. "I can't wait."

There was nothing they could do there so they decided to get back home. As they were walking away, Jim kept looking over his shoulder, toward the burning house. His expression was pained and angry. When the roof caved in, there was a loud crash causing all of them to stop and turn to watch the carnage. The last semblance of what had been a loving, happy home collapsed before their eyes. Jim let a tear run down his cheek as the flames roared, engulfing the remnants of the roof, feeding the greedy appetite of the fire. He wiped his face, set his jaw, and turned back toward home—their new home.

"Four walls and a roof. Without a family in it that's all it is. Home is where your heart is, where your loved ones are. We all got a new one now. New home and a new family. Guess we'd best get back to it." Jim headed for the farm. He didn't turn around again.

****

Alan and Rich watched from the edge of the trees as the guys headed out on foot. He slammed his hand against the nearest one, causing Rich to jump. After much berating from Alan, he had gotten out of the truck and joined him.

"Dammit! They're walking! I just knew they'd open the gate and drive over there. We don't know any more now than we did before, except they have at least five guys. You can bet your ass there's more inside. Dammit!" Alan hissed this under his breath to Rich, who appeared to be trying desperately to bear his pain in silence.

"So, what now, Al? We heading out to find more guys then? They for sure got us outnumber two to one. Could be three to one or more. What do you want to do?" The act of speaking caused him more pain but he gritted his teeth and grimaced through it.

"We got no choice but to go find more guys. C'mon, get in the truck. We gotta go pick up Steve and get to lookin'."

Rich, thankful to be going back to the truck where he could rest again, nodded and followed Alan, then hesitated. "But, those guys are headed to where Steve is. Aren't we gonna wait 'til they come back before we go head that way?"

"Nah, I figured we'd drive right up on 'em over there. Of course, we're not goin' straight back there, you idiot. We're gonna wait down the road from the *fire* place 'til they leave. Get it? *Fire* place? Hahahahahaha! I crack myself up!"

Rich gave Alan a half-hearted grin and climbed in the cab, grateful for the cushioning. "Yer a riot, Al, that's for sure."

Alan was still laughing at his own wit as he pulled out onto the road. "Fire place. Ha!"

Chapter 5

Gary awoke to a loud banging on the front door. He had no idea what time it was, since his digital watch got fried in the pulse, but he could see the sun coming through the blinds over the window in his office. He got up, grabbed his pants, boots, and gun belt, and headed out front. There appeared to be at least a dozen people at the door. *What now?* he thought as he hopped into his boots. He unlocked the door and opened it wide.

"Morning, folks. What can I do for you?"

A large man named Doug stepped forward, apparently acting as spokesman for the group. "Sheriff, we need to know what the government is gonna do about feeding folks around here. Everybody is out of food and there ain't no stores selling any. Isn't that something tax dollars are used for? Didn't the government plan for something like this? It's been weeks since everything went off. Y'all got some way to contact Washington, I'm sure. We need to declare a state of emergency or something if that ain't been done yet. This is one of those situations they've been preparing for with that Homeland Security crap, ain't it? Where is the National Guard with supplies to help out? We know the mayor has been stayin' here, and we want to hear from her what's being done to take care of the people of this town. That's her job. That's your job, too. We need to feed our kids. And don't give us any of that *'we're workin' on it'* bullshit either. We need food now. So, what are you gonna do about it?"

Gary took in the expectant faces looking at him. He'd been waiting for this and was actually surprised they had taken this long to show up. He had to handle this situation tactfully. The last thing he needed was an angry, hungry mob going after the mayor or himself. He addressed the group as a whole. "I know y'all are in need. We're working on a couple of different plans to grow food for the town. But that's not an overnight thing. You know it takes weeks, even months, for some plants to grow to harvest. In the meantime, I'd suggest you all pool your resources. If you can help each other—"

A woman from the back cut him off. "What do ya think we've *been* doin'? We ain't had nothing but chicken broth and liquid Jell-O for a week or more at our house! We ain't got no more resources to *pool*, Sheriff! The last soup I made was more like water that a chicken walked past. There is nothing left in my cupboards. Not a grain of rice, not a pinto bean to be seen. My kids ain't eat in two days, and it's been closer to four for me. We need food *now!*" She shouted the last word, and the crowd rallied around her with their own cries.

Gary waited for the group to calm down some, then spoke again in an even tone. "I understand. I want to help. I'm trying to set things in motion for all of our futures. We don't know what's going on with Washington. We haven't heard anything. We don't have any magic contact with the outside world. We lost everything the same as you all did. The only things we know are what has been told to us by folks with ham radios. If they weren't plugged in, a lot of them made it through the pulse. No one has reported seeing anything even remotely resembling our government or our aid agencies. And, in all likelihood, we won't. We're just a small community of about a thousand people now. If there are any branches of the government still operating, they will be focusing on big cities with hundreds of thousands, or even millions, of people. The needs of the many, as they say. Honestly, I don't think anyone from our government is doing anything to help the people of this country. And no one knows how long this is going to last. It could take months, even years, to get the power back."

At that, the crowd roared again.

"Years? We'll all be dead by then!"

"How are we supposed to live that long without power?"

"What are we going to do?"

Gary held his hands up for quiet. As soon as they complied, he went on. "I am working on a plan with one of the farmers in the area who still has equipment running. He agreed to let us farm a section of his place for the town. There's a couple of old artesian wells just outside of town we can haul water in for folks to use. But that's still not an overnight fix. Since no one has anything at all, we have some emergency rations that we can hand out. It will only be enough for one meal a day per person, and only for three days. However, in that time, I want the names of at least six men or women who hunt—successfully." There were a few laughs from the crowd, whose eyes lit up at the prospect of a meal.

Doug broke in. "Where are these rations, Sheriff? How come you ain't offered them before now?"

Gary looked Doug in the eye. "One, we don't have many. Two, because of that, we needed it to be a dire emergency, because, three, I refer you back to one. It's not a fix. It's barely a Band-Aid. That's why I want hunters who will agree to hunt for a community food larder. That should help ease some of the hunger pangs."

The group of townsfolk seemed to like the idea of getting food. There were small smiles and nods. Gary continued. "This is not free food we're working on. Everybody—every adult and every child over thirteen—will be expected to contribute in some way. The thirteen-year-olds can watch the kids whose parents are working the crops. We gathered all the available seeds at the co-op, and have sorted them out by how fast they grow. Everyone with a yard will be required to dig it up to plant food. We can have leafy greens like arugula and lettuce, as well as radishes, in less than thirty days. Spinach and bush beans in forty-five to fifty. In two months, we can have turnips and cucumbers. That's a nice variety of veggies right there, y'all."

A man named Ben spoke up from the center of the group. "How do you know all that about how long it takes them plants to grow, Sheriff? You a farmer, too?"

Gary smiled at him. "I'd love to tell you I am, Ben, but no, I've never grown anything but a yard. But I can read. I looked at the seed packets, and grabbed some books from the library on gardening. They'll be available to anyone who wants to use them. We all need to know how to grow food now."

Another woman asked, "But, if we have a piece of farm land we can work and use for growing things, why do we have to dig up our yards to plant vegetables? Do you have any idea how much money we spent on sod for our yard last year?"

Ben turned and looked at her. "Unless you're planning on eating that pretty grass, I'd say yeah, you need to dig it up."

The crowd laughed as the woman turned red with embarrassment. Gary grinned at Ben, then looked at the crowd. "Exactly. We need food and lots of it. Besides, it's not like you can mow your lawn now. Might as well put that spot to a valuable use. By the way, the money you paid for that nice lawn won't entirely go to waste. The soil should be in really good shape for growing vegetables."

Angie stepped through the door Gary was holding open. She had been listening to the conversations and was ready to address a portion of her people. "Folks, there will be a town meeting at noon today in the square. We are going to lay out the plans for right now, and then for longer term. Please help us spread the word. Anybody who wants to eat any time soon needs to be there. We'll answer any questions we can. Thank you all for coming. Please go tell your neighbors about the meeting, and we'll see you all then. Sheriff? Can I speak to you for a moment?" She inclined her head at him, and he nodded.

Gary was turning to go inside when Doug accosted him. "What about them rations, Sheriff? I thought we was getting them now." There were murmurings of dissent among the group.

Gary replied, "Rations will be distributed at the meeting. Anyone who needs them will get them then."

Doug retorted, "But we're hungry now!" Several others in the crowd began raising their voices to join him.

"I know you are. Lots of folks are. But we have to be fair to everyone. Again, they'll be handed out at the meeting. Now, please go spread the word." Gary turned and closed the office door, making a point of loudly turning the deadbolt. He looked at Angie. "I sure hope this doesn't turn into a riot when we start giving out those rations."

She looked at him resolutely. "It won't, because the first thing we are going to tell them is that if it does, no one gets anything. You should probably have a couple more deputies though. Any word from the other ones under your employ? Did they ever get in, or try to contact you?"

He shook his head. "Sheila and Randy were seeing each other, although they didn't want anyone to know, since if that got out, I'd have to let one of them go. From the rumors I heard, they were staying out at his place most of the time, which was on the very edge of the county. Another half mile and he wouldn't have been eligible to work here. By the time I got out there, there was no one anywhere to be seen. It was probably a good week and a half after everything went down. I have no idea what became of them."

Angie had a sad look on her face. "Well, if we haven't heard anything by now, we can only imagine the worst. One would hope that a couple of sheriff's deputies might be able to make it in this world, but nothing is certain, is it?"

Gary closed his eyes for a moment, then looked at her. "No, it sure isn't. Marry me, Angie."

Angie went from sad to shocked. "What? Did you just ask me to marry you? Where did that come from, Gary?"

He glanced at the door and saw there were still people outside, so he took her hand and led her around the corner into his office. He wrapped her in his arms and stared into her eyes. "From my heart, that's where. We aren't guaranteed anything in this world, especially now. I love you. I have for a long time. We've been dancing around each other for months, hell, years, and I'm tired of it. If we only have a month, or a year, or ten years, that's fine by me. Say yes, darlin'."

Angie melted at that sweet expression and smiled, a smile that lit up her whole face. "Yes, I'll marry you. Now, when would we …"

"Today. In the square, in front of everyone. The first preacher I see gets the pleasure of making you Mrs. Angie Burns."

"Well, um, okay then. I better go see if I have a clean skirt." With that, she leaned up to him and closed her eyes. He met her halfway with a kiss that took her breath away. When they came up for air, she grinned at him. "Yeah, let's make this quick. I want more of that and … other stuff."

He laughed out loud and picked her up in his arms. Just then, Tim walked in the door. "Oh shit, I'm sorry Sheriff. I didn't mean to interrupt—"

Gary put Angie back on her feet. "No problem, Tim. You'll be the first to hear the news. Angie and I are getting married. Today. In the town square at the meeting."

"What meeting?" Tim seemed slightly put off at that, probably that something had been planned that he wasn't included in. He didn't even acknowledge the wedding announcement.

Angie addressed him. "We are getting the townsfolk together to lay out the plans for growing food here in town and out at the Warren place. Everyone is going to have to pitch in and do their part if we are to have a chance of not starving this winter. We're also going to hand out three meals from the emergency rations here to the most needy people, to try to tide them over until we can get some real food coming into town."

Tim didn't even try to hide the disdain on his face. "No offense, Mayor Hale, but what is three meals going to do to help anyone? That's one day. What about tomorrow, and the next day? They'll just come back for more, and probably not too politely. We'll have a riot on our hands for whatever is left."

"There won't be anything left, Deputy. We're distributing it all."

"*What*? Are you crazy? What are we supposed to eat then?"

Angie looked him in the eye. "The same thing everyone else does. Whatever we can grow or hunt. The free food train is pulling out of the station, Tim. We're all in this mess together and we lead by example. Now excuse me, I have to go find something decent to get married in. I'll see you fellas later."

Angie walked out of the office. Tim stared after her, then turned on Gary. "Sheriff, you can't do this. We need those supplies. How can we protect the town with no food to keep us going?"

Gary looked at Tim with disgust. "Protect the town, Tim? The only thing you've protected since this whole thing started is your own interests. You looked out for you and no one else. That stops today. Angie's right. We have to send the message that we are no better than anyone else in town, and will be working just as hard as they are to get by. Part of our job, besides helping with the food stores, will be protecting the people and our supplies from marauders. Once we get some food laid by, we'll need round the clock security to protect it. I intend to deputize about a half dozen people to help with that. We also still need to get out to the Callen place and see if those men are still there. I doubt it, I mean that would be stupid to stay there knowing we'd find out from Clay where they were, but I wouldn't take them as particularly smart. Unfortunately, that will have to wait. We need to get these rations handed out. Some of those folks are in real bad shape. Start boxing up anything that's not already packed. And don't even think about stashing any for yourself. I know almost to the pack how much food and water is here. It all goes."

Tim turned without another word and headed for the break room.

****

When the items were counted, there was enough for three meals for a day for twenty-five hundred people. Rough guesses put the current population in town at around a thousand, but there were a lot of trailer parks and small subdivisions just outside the city limits. Angie stretched her back and looked around the room.

"I believe we can help some people a little here. If we can get the farm going quickly, maybe get some community hunters lined up for those folks that don't know how, we might be able to make it. Once the crops start coming in, I think we should put half to three-quarters of it back—anything that can be canned, and possibly dehydrated, and even smoke or sugar-cured meats. Perhaps Barbara Manchin has some room in her basement to hang country hams. We'll just have to see what the need is, how many people we'll be providing for …"

She paused, seeming to gather her thoughts. Tim asked, "Do you really think we can help anybody with just three meals? One day's worth of food is nothing. All you're going to do is make them hungry for more."

Angie sighed. "Tim, I'm trying very hard to understand your actions thus far in this catastrophe. The survival mode is a very powerful part of our makeup. I get that you want to survive. Seriously, if you only want to look out for yourself, feel free to walk out that door and go hunting. *That* meat, *that* food would be yours to do with as you please. *This*," she waved her hand to the rations, "is not. All of it belongs to the community. The only reason we don't open the doors and invite people in to take it is they would act exactly the way you have. They would take as much as they could and hoard it. The slower among them would get nothing. So, we have to meter it so that it is spread out equally. What you get on your own is yours. What belonged to the town is everyone's. I believe you have been more than compensated for protecting these provisions up to this point." She crossed her arms and waited for his response.

Tim eyed the rations then looked from her to Gary. "Exactly how am I supposed to perform my duties with nothing to eat? I can't protect and serve with no food."

Gary looked thoughtful, then replied, "Can you hunt?"

"Yeah. I haven't since I was a kid though. My grandpa took me."

Gary nodded. "It's been a while for me, too. Tell you what. We'll take turns hunting each morning. Take my truck out toward the east. There's a lot less people living that direction, so hopefully there will be less competition. Squirrel, rabbit, a deer if we're lucky; that would feed us for a few days. We'll work together to feed those of us here. I'm going to the library today to see if there are any books on wild edible plants and living off the land. I know you can use every part of a cattail, but I don't know how to do it. There's dandelions everywhere and I know for a fact we can eat those. I just don't know what all the edible plants are or what they look like, but I'll know soon. We'll share that knowledge with the folks in town, too. We can do this, Tim, but we have to work together, all of us. Are you willing to try?"

Tim didn't answer at first. He considered what Gary had said. After a moment, he took a deep breath, stood tall and answered, "Ya know, I think I am, Sheriff. I've been looking for the easy way my whole life. I hung out with the wrong people growing up. Getting on with the department is the best thing I ever did, even though I still wanted to find the path that took me the least amount of work. Looks like everyone is gonna be doing a lot of work now. Being a deputy is something I love, and I think I'm good at. I want to help. I would ask that you let me keep on staying here. My house is ten miles away and I don't have a vehicle that runs. If I stay here, I'll be close if I'm needed in town."

Gary smiled. "Yes, that's fine. I'll be staying, too. My house is further out than yours. No sense burning gas if we don't have to. That will run out eventually just like everything else. We'll need every drop for transporting folks to the farm to work the crops—if there's still a farm to go to."

Tim felt a twinge of guilt at the fact that he knew the men who had caused that problem. At one point in his life, he had called them friends. Now, he realized they were traveling down two different roads. Theirs was a road of evil intent. He might even have joined them not too long ago. But now, his road was going to take him toward being a better person, a value to his community, a trusted deputy protecting the people of his town. That sounded a whole lot better than wanted killer. Safer too.

****

"How many of you know how to preserve and keep food without refrigeration?" Angie broached the question to the crowd of about two hundred people in the small park beside the courthouse. A dozen or so of the attendees raised their hands, mostly older

64

women, but a few men and a couple of younger people. Angie nodded at them with a satisfied smile on her face. "I would like some of you to volunteer to teach classes on your chosen method of food preservation to others in town. I'm assuming we're talking about canning, possibly making jerky, those types of things. Are there others?"

An older man named Clint raised his hand. "I know how to salt cure meat."

"Excellent. Anyone else with alternative methods?"

"How about smoking meat? That ain't the same as making jerky," another gentleman spoke up from the back.

A woman beside him replied, "And dehydrating fruits and vegetables. Not exactly the same as making jerky either. But also, not as easy to do without electricity to power a dehydrator."

Angie went on. "Perfect. I'm sure by now you've all figured out that life as we knew it is gone for the foreseeable future. We have had no contact with any government entities. I think it's pretty safe to say we are on our own. With no electricity, we need to use alternative methods to preserve food for months, possibly years."

Another woman with two small children at her side and one on her hip, all looking as if they hadn't bathed since the pulse, commented aloud. "What food? There ain't no more food. It's all gone. The stores are empty. Where are we supposed to get this food? Hell, if you know where some is I ain't interested in preserving it. I need to feed my kids. We ain't had a bite to eat in two days."

Angie addressed her directly. "I understand your concern. We are working on some arrangements with local farmers right now to try to get some crops planted as soon as possible. We just have to hold on—"

She was interrupted by a portly man. "Hold on? With what? Sally there just told you—there ain't no food nowhere. No food, no water, at least none you could drink without killing yourself. But you look like you're in pretty good shape, Mayor. Don't look like you're doin' without …"

Clint was standing next to the man and patted his protruding stomach. "Don't look like you're doin' too bad either, Silas. I don't see any new holes cut in your belt. What's your secret? You got a tunnel to Ms. Loretta's root cellar next door to ya?"

Everyone laughed, including spunky eighty-year-old Loretta King, who then replied, "No he don't, and if he tried he'd likely be shot." More laughs came from the group, except for Silas who looked angry, probably at being the butt of back-to-back jokes. "I shared what I had canned up over the past few years with him and pert near every other house on our block, so my canned goods are gone as well. Mayor Hale, you get me some stuff to can and I'll be more than happy to teach other folks how to do it. Lord knows there ain't many young people nowadays that know how to get through life without pizza deliveries, or microwaves for their cooking, and houses with electrical doodads that talk to you. Everybody's gotta learn what it takes to survive without all that now."

Loretta's comments were met with murmurs and nods. Angie's smile returned. "Thank you so much, Miss Loretta, for your generosity to your neighbors and your offer to teach others the very valuable skills you have. Yes, we all have to learn what it takes to live without the luxuries and amenities we had before. Anyone willing to share their knowledge and experience of any useful skills—not just food related—with others, please come see me after the meeting. Anyone who wants to learn how to perform one of these jobs, see me as well. We will be hauling water into town from the artesian wells. Please gather suitable containers to hold it to take to your homes. We'd like to keep it to a gallon per person per day to save on gas hauling it in. Everyone is going to have to participate in some way for a share of the food we will be growing and storing, as well as eating through the summer, fall, winter, and into next spring. If you don't help, you don't eat. There's no free ride. Now, our next order of bus—"

She was interrupted by Silas again. "Before you get on to your next order of business, Mayor, we ain't quite done with the food issue. We heard there was going to be rations handed out at this meeting, three days' worth. Three meals a day for three days is nine meals. We want our nine meals."

Angie started to reply but Gary stepped forward and placed a hand on her arm. She looked at him and nodded, then took a step back.

"Silas, I'm afraid you have been misinformed. We don't have that many supplies. It's three meals, with water. You can, and should, try to stretch that out over three days, because once those are gone, that's it. That's why we need hunters right now willing to go out and hunt for a community food bank. But we also need people to process the meat, and dole it out fairly. The work starts today, people. We hope the meager rations will help you get a bit of strength back so you can contribute because, like Mayor Hale said, if you don't help, you don't eat. If you work, you'll get an equal share."

Silas's eyes grew wide. "Three meals? Why, that's not even enough to start to make up for not eating regular for the past month! We need more than that!"

Gary looked him in the eye. "Three meals per person. That's it. And if there's any trouble, any semblance of anything other than an orderly group of people patiently waiting their turn to receive those meals, we will shut it down and no one will get anything. Is that understood, Silas?"

At Gary's remarks, three men stepped up beside him wearing deputy badges. Jasper Jenkins, Ben Vaughn, and of course, Tim Miller, were watching the crowd closely for any signs of disruption. Silas said nothing, but gave the sheriff a short nod of assent.

"Good. My last order of business is to announce that right after the rations are handed out, Reverend Walters is going to perform a wedding ceremony for Angie Hale and myself. You're all welcome to stay and witness it. Thank you."

There were shouts and whistles and lots of hand clapping. Gary turned to Angie with a wink and a grin. She smiled back at him then took center stage again. "Thank you, thank you all. Please form a line at the table on the left for rations and the table on the right for both teachers and students, as well as hunters who will hunt for the community. Anyone who is not in one of those categories after today will be expected to devote the majority of their time to gardening, either at your home or at the community garden once the location is finalized. If you have any other concerns, feel free to come see me later."

The crowd had started moving, mostly toward the rations table, when Gary thought of another item the townspeople needed to be aware of. "People, one more thing. There are some bad folks out on the road now. They will kill you for anything you may or may not have if they think it might be valuable. That includes food, water, medications, jewelry, guns, ammo, and unfortunately women and kids. Keep your doors locked. Do not let anyone in you don't know. If you have one, keep your gun close and your family closer. Check on your neighbors when you can. My team can't be everywhere, so we're going to have to rely on you all to protect yourselves and each other. Word will get out that we have food and drinking water. If nothing else, those two things are what every desperate person out there will be looking for. Be careful. Be smart. Stay safe."

He turned away from the crowd and Ben got his attention. "Women and kids? What for?"

Gary gave him a pained look. One that said, "Don't make me say it out loud." Ben looked confused, then his face changed as the realization of what it meant set in. It became a look of horror, disgust, and finally rage.

"*Kids*? They're raping *kids*?"

Gary patted his hand in the air to Ben. "Keep your voice down, Ben. I'm sure others will figure that part out as well, but let's try not to get everyone riled up, at least until we get through this ration handout. Why don't you go over and keep an eye on that."

"Sorry, Gary. Sure thing." Ben walked away, mumbling to himself.

Jasper watched him, walking over to where Gary stood. "I'm gonna sign up for the hunters as well, Gary. My old truck still runs, so I can probably take a few folks with me on hunts. We'll be heavy on meat until we can get some of them greens grown, but we'll live. I can lend a small generator for running dehydrators if you can supply the gas. Got some pretty good jerky recipes as long as the spices hold out."

Gary perked up. "Hell yeah, we can get gas, but we need the generator to get it out of the ground. Vicious circle there. Spices we may be able to help on. Not a lot of looting on the spice aisle."

Jasper laughed. "We can siphon some gas out of dead cars if we need to for the genny. Let's get together later and work out the details."

"Thanks, Jasper. Come by the office later this afternoon. Right now, I gotta go see a man about a wedding."

Chapter 6

After the deaths of Bill and Pete, we had to face the fact that we were not as safe as we had thought. Not safe at all. We felt we were vulnerable now. Monroe rescinded the offer to the sheriff of the use of the land, when he came back a few days later. That he would go against what Millie wanted, which was to give them another chance, said a lot about his feelings toward the matter. Yet, Gary still tried to get him to change his mind.

"Monroe, I know this is bad, but we can still make it work. Everybody in town isn't like those guys who did this to your people. No one even knows them. There are folks back there who really want to—"

"I don't give a rat's ass what they want, Gary! We were trying to do a good thing, trying to help our fellow man, and what did it get us? Two of our people dead, and we hadn't even got started yet! No, no one is going to be allowed on this property for anything unless we expressly invite them in and I don't see that happening for anyone else any time soon. Or maybe ever. Most likely never."

Gary shook his head. "Monroe, we can provide protection for you and your folks here, 24/7 if need be. Hell, I'll put up a tent and stay here all the time if I have to for this to be a viable option. No one in town has the experience with growing large crops that you do. No one there has the equipment you have, especially any still running. You're one of the few farmers here in the area with working vehicles and machinery. This is about feeding other families that will starve before winter even gets here, much less when it does. I know this is going to last for a while. I'm trying to help as many people as I can get prepared for it."

Monroe crossed his arms and set his jaw. "Then you'd best get busy looking for an alternative plan and location. It ain't gonna be here."

The sheriff's shoulders sagged as he started to turn away. "You can use my place," Jim said.

Gary's head snapped up. "Seriously, Jim? You'd do that?"

Jim shrugged. "It's not like we can live there now, even if the power did come back on. The house is gone. Might as well use the land to help folks if we can. My tractor doesn't run though. It's too new. You'll still need Monroe's equipment. Good thing is the rows had already been done before everything went off. There's even some stuff planted you can take when it comes up. Early spring plants like kale, lettuce, radishes, carrots, that kind of thing. Oh, and there's a couple of rows of potatoes in the ground. We were planning to go back from time to time to harvest, but with the gardens we have here, we can let those over there go to someone else. It'll make Charlotte happy to know she's helping out her neighbors."

Gary was grinning from ear to ear. "Jim, that's awesome! On behalf of the townsfolk, thank you! And whether your house is there or not, I'll still provide protection for the place. How many acres do you have worked already?"

"Probably only about one. We weren't planning to feed more than the five of us. There's another four or so clear that is usable for a garden. But as I said, you'll need Monroe's tractor to get it ready."

With that, everyone turned to Monroe, who was still in his defensive stance. With a scowl, he mumbled, "I reckon we can do that much. If nothin' else, it'll get Millie off my back about *not helpin'* my fellow man. But the first sign of any more trouble and we're done, Sheriff. You understand?"

Gary was still grinning and now nodding vigorously. "Absolutely, absolutely. When can we get started?"

Jim was shouldering his pack. "We can go now if you want, Gary. I'll ride over with you."

Ryan stepped up to them. "I'll go, too. None of our people go anywhere alone, remember?"

Jim looked at him and smiled. "I won't exactly be alone, Ryan. The sheriff will be with me."

Ryan walked toward Gary's truck. He stopped, slowly turned around and replied, "He's not one of us." He turned to the truck and climbed in the back, scanning the area, rifle at the ready.

The sheriff looked to Monroe who shrugged and said, "He's right. You ain't." With that, he headed back through the gate.

The rest of us followed, Bob bringing up the rear. He walked up to Gary, and with a sidelong glance at Ryan said quietly, "Keep an eye on him, Sheriff. He's in a bad place right now. It's almost like he's looking for trouble, mainly with those assholes that killed his brother, Bill. I don't blame him, mind you, but we're all worried about him. Ya know what I mean?"

Gary nodded and gave Bob a grim smile. "I hear ya, and I'll try to watch out for him. We went looking for those guys, but they weren't at the Callen place anymore. I hate it took me so long to get back out here but it's been hell in town. Folks are out of food, they have no clean water, and they're pretty much in panic mode. I can't even begin to describe the shape they left Luke and Casey's house in. I haven't had the heart to tell them yet. That and I don't want him going off half-cocked looking for those guys for payback. We'll find them. I've got my deputy, Tim, on that as we speak. They will answer for what they've done."

"Let's hope so - for all our sakes, but especially our folks who lost their kin. We're trying to save that young man out there … from himself." With that, Bob reached out to shake Gary's hand.

Gary gave him a firm handshake, smiled, and turned to head to his truck. He stopped when Bob called his name.

"Sheriff Burns? About you finding them and making them pay for what they've done? You better hurry, because if our folks find them first …" He didn't finish. Gary nodded grimly at him.

"I hear ya. Two months ago, I would have admonished all of you about taking the law into your own hands. Problem is, there isn't much law left, and there's only one of me. I can't say I'd blame any of you for doing my job for me."

Gary touched the brim of his cap and got into his truck. As he turned around to head out to Jim's, Bob looked at Russ. "I can't believe he said that, or that I agree with it, but I do. And I almost hope we find those scumbags before he does."

Russ watched them leave. "Either way, it's going to be a bad situation, buddy."

Bob solemnly replied, "It already is, brother."

****

Gary was very excited about the prospects of the Dotson farm. He walked the area a few times, mentally laying out crops. He looked at Jim and grinned. "Jim, this is great! How much food can we grow here? How many people can we feed, and how long will it feed them?"

Jim replied, "Well, I read somewhere that if you planted the right stuff, at the right time, you could get an average of around ten thousand pounds of food off an acre of land. With five acres, that would be close to fifty thousand pounds. You could possibly get another crop of some of the stuff that is frost resistant, like broccoli, cabbage, carrots, onions, most of the leafy vegetables like greens and lettuces, even some peas. Heck, you can keep spinach going all summer and into the winter. So, if you planted the whole thing again once the first crops were out, you're looking at twice that. I'm guessing you're gonna supplement this food with hunting and fishing?"

Gary was ticking off numbers in his head. *One hundred thousand pounds of food, for a thousand people, give or take, that's a hundred pounds per person. Not much to last a year, or at least until next spring. But, with the addition of game and livestock meat, maybe it would be enough. They'd have to cook smart, make soups that would feed a lot of folks with a minimum amount of ingredients ...*

Jim interrupted Gary's train of thought. "Sheriff? You still with me?"

"What? Sorry, Jim, I was doing some calculating. It sounds like a ton of food—fifty tons actually—but when you divide it over a thousand people, it really isn't. Yes, we'll add meat through hunting, fishing, and bartering for livestock when we can, but those aren't guarantees. Looks like we're gonna need folks to plant their whole yards as well."

Jim nodded. "Seems like that shouldn't even be a question. A good-looking lawn is nice but you can't make a meal of it, unless you're a cow or a goat or some other critter."

Gary nodded. "Yep, we had almost that exact same discussion with some folks in town who were concerned about digging up their expensive lawns to plant food. We're just going to have to work every available plot we can. I think there are some tillers at the co-op. Those should still run."

"Well, we can test that right now. I bought one from there last year. Hadn't thought to try it 'til now. It's out back in the shed."

Ryan had been standing with them, listening and scanning the area constantly. "You guys go ahead. I'll keep watch out here."

Jim laid a hand on his shoulder. "Alright, son, holler if you see anything that ain't supposed to be here."

Ryan gave a curt nod and wandered across the yard. Jim watched him for a moment, then turned to Gary. "Let's go see about that tiller now."

****

Ryan was walking through the tall grass of a once well-kept lawn. *No one is mowing in the apocalypse, no matter what it looks like on TV shows.* He smiled slightly at the thought. It was something he and Bill had always commented on when watching zombie shows.

"Why is that grass short? The zombies have been there for years now. No one mows during a zombie apocalypse!" He'd comment on it every time. Bill would grin at him and come back with something like, "Figures someone who mows yards for a living would notice something like that. I'm pretty sure no one would pay for our services if that happened, little brother, so I sure as hell ain't mowing." Ryan would then laugh along with Bill as they contemplated life in an apocalyptic world. *It's nothing like we thought it would be, big brother, and I sure expected you to be here with me.* He closed his eyes, took a deep breath, and continued on to the tree line.

As he was scanning the area, he noticed something on the ground under an ornamental bush. Crouching down, he pushed the leafy branches out of the way so he could see the ground. He saw a couple of cigarette butts laying there. He climbed into the spot and sat down. Looking around, he found he had a perfect view of the yard, house, and driveway.

"Son of a bitch!" he yelled. "They were here! One of them was right here!"

At the sound of his raised voice, Gary and Jim came running around the side of the shed and the burned-out hull of the house. Gary was drawing his sidearm. "What is it? Who's here? Where are they?"

Ryan crawled out of the spot behind the bush. "No one's here now. At least one of those bastards was right here in this spot, probably watching us the whole time we were looking for them after the fire. Look!" He pointed to the cigarette butts and the slightly cleared spot under the bush. Jim peered in.

"None of us smoke, so it makes sense it was one of them. Damn it! I sure woulda liked to have gotten my hands on one of them bastards that burned the house down."

Ryan looked at Jim, then Gary. "Not half as much as I want to put a bullet in them."

Gary's face showed no emotion. "I hear you, Ryan. I understand you're hurting. You have every right to feel the way you do. I just hope you don't end up doing something you'll regret the rest of your life because of the pain you're feeling right now."

Ryan stared at him. "I don't regret shooting the one I did. I won't regret finishing off the rest of them either. Don't worry about me, Sheriff. Worry about them. We ready to head back?"

Gary nodded slowly, watching Ryan. "Yes, the tiller worked so we can pretty much bet the others will too. Let's get you fellas home and me back to town. I've got a lot of work ahead of me today."

They loaded back into Gary's truck, Ryan in the bed surveilling all around. *I've got a lot of work ahead of me, too. Maybe not today, but soon. I'll find you, all of you. And when I do, you're dead.*

Chapter 7

Jasper knocked on the back door of the old store. "Barbara? You in there? I've got work for you."

Barbara threw on her robe and house shoes, shuffled down the stairs to the back door, peered through the peephole she had installed a few weeks ago, unlocked and opened the door, presenting him with a scowl and a squint at the early morning sunlight. "Jasper! Do you know what time it is? I wasn't planning to be up for at least another hour. I was up late last night trying to catch up on the meat I had that needed processing. What in heaven's name is so damn important you couldn't wait until I put out the sign saying I was working, and that you'd take the chance of waking up the kids?"

Jasper grinned at her. "This." He stepped aside to reveal two big deer, a doe and a buck, in the bed of his old pickup truck. "I was only after him, but she stepped up not too long after I got him, right in my path coming out of the woods, so I figured I was supposed to get her, too. Since I was so fortunate, and I only have to donate one to the town's stores, I'll up your payment from a quarter to a third of the doe meat on this deal. I was worried it might get too warm today, so I wanted to get them to you early, so you can get 'em downstairs where it's cooler."

At the offer of a higher payment, Barbara grinned, rubbed the sleep from her eyes, and opened the door wider. "Well, c'mon then. Let's get them critters downstairs. I'll unlock the basement door and meet you over there—right after I get some coffee brewing. Looks like it's gonna be a busy day for me."

Jasper nodded, rubbing his hands together. "Mm mm, two deer and coffee, too? This is my lucky day."

Barbara cocked her head at him. "Did I say I was making coffee for you, mister? I don't recall saying that. Wait, let me think a minute …"

Jasper pouted. "Oh, now don't tease me like that, Barb. I've been out of coffee for weeks. You know it's evil to make coffee and not offer it to your company, who can smell it, and almost taste it, and—"

Barbara laughed at him. "Fine, fine, quit yer whinin'. I guess you can have a cup. But only one, since I'm getting low, and I ran out of cream yesterday. Maybe someone will have some milk to trade today for a bit of tasty venison."

"Only if you get somebody from outside of town. Townsfolk don't have cows. Maybe some chickens. Maybe. If they haven't eaten them yet."

Barbara lost her smile and nodded solemnly. "Yes, unfortunately the pangs of hunger outweigh the smarter choice of letting the animals breed to make more for food. Fortunately, though, the folks out in the country know those kinds of things and won't eat their future food resources. Say, how are you coming on getting me fixed up to keep a freezer running? How's that windmill set up coming along, or whatever it is? If I can keep the meat longer, I don't have to rush to get it traded off. At full capacity, with everything frozen solid, I only have to run the freezer maybe a couple of hours a day. That big generator works great, but I'm getting dangerously low on gas. I doubt it will make it the rest of the week."

Jasper went to his truck. "Glad you asked. I'm not completely ready with the wind turbine generator, still got a few kinks to work out, but I found this over at the hardware store. Had to trade a little .380 pistol and a box of ammo to get it." He held up a round part with hoses, bolts, and other pieces in the bag.

"What is it?" Barbara asked as she inspected the item.

"It's a conversion kit for the generator. We install this and the generator will be able to use propane, or even natural gas, in place of regular gasoline. There are plenty of empty houses with gas grills in the backyard around here. Lots of folks don't think to scavenge that kind of gas. Plus, I think there are a bunch of hundred-pound tanks at the co-op. We can fill a few from their storage tanks and bring them here. That should last you long enough for me to work something out on the turbine."

"That's great! I may throw in a second cup of coffee for that. See ya on the other side." She winked at him, then went to the kitchen to start the camp stove she was cooking on, and get the coffee pot going. After that was done, she headed for the basement. The outside entrance was locked from the inside with two heavy duty hasps held closed by extremely large locks. She had found evidence early on of someone trying to break in that way and added a second, as well as a brand new one to replace the one her dad had installed years ago to "keep honest people honest, and keep the thievin' assholes out." She smiled at the memory of her father from her youth and thanked his spirit once again for teaching her a skill she could use and, even more important, was viable and valued in this strange new world.

She was removing the second lock as Jasper backed up to the door. He got out and grabbed a rope from the bed. He tied one end around the buck's back legs and threw the other to Barbara. "If we can, I'd like to save the skin. Amanda is gearing up to tan hides for leather for shoes, tool handles, that sort of thing. Her granddad, Luke, has forgotten more about tanning than all of us put together know. We're damn lucky he's still around to help her, although she knows quite a bit already. He's been teaching it to her for years. She did it as a hobby before, but being a computer programmer isn't going to put food on the table these days. Hell, being an electrician isn't much better. I'm having to dig deep in my memory for how to make things run without being able to plug them into the nearest outlet. That's why the turbine is taking so long. I have to scrounge for parts that aren't fried to make it work."

"Well, if you need parts, you know where you have to go to find them. Monroe has a little bit of everything at his place." She was threading the rope into one hook on a come-along she had overhead, attached to a slide rail that ran the length of the basement. Her dad had installed it for this very purpose. She put a tarp on the ground to keep from scuffing the hide when the carcass came off the truck bed.

Jasper was trying to keep the buck from sliding off before the rope got taut. "Yeah, you're right, I need to get out there and see if he has what we need for your power to keep running. You being able to use your electric saws and grinders is the difference between meat for a few folks every day or meat for a lot of folks instead. Good thing you kept those old pieces of your dad's equipment, since the newer ones got fried in the pulse."

"Had I known there was going to be an electrical apocalypse, I would have unplugged everything that night. Live and learn."

Jasper chuckled at her sarcasm. "Yeah, I lost quite a bit of equipment myself. Had to go back old school. I found some books at the library, in the vintage section, that had a lot of info I can use. Vintage is the world we live in now."

"Tell me about it. My dad's old meat saw and grinder are a godsend. Good thing I stuck them in a corner instead of the trash when I got the new equipment a few years ago. Well, let's get these guys hung up. I'll start on them after I get some caffeine in me. Yep, it's gonna be a busy day."

****

The butcher shop had been Barbara Manchin's childhood home. She grew up in an apartment above it with her parents and younger brother, Zach. Both of her parents had passed on, and her little brother was living out west on a cattle ranch. She thought about him almost daily, hoping he was alive and surviving in these crazy times. If nothing else, he was in a place without a lot of people, and with a lot of food.

While many such businesses had shut down with the advent of big chain supermarkets and big box stores, Manchin's Meats had survived. There was a loyal customer base of folks in town who liked knowing how their meat was processed, without fillers and additives. Barbara also processed game for the hunters in the area, as her father had done before her. It wasn't that the hunters couldn't do it. Any hunter worth their salt could process their own kills. It was because she did it so fast and packaged everything neatly, ready to go in the freezer. She also had a secret recipe for venison summer sausage passed down to her by her dad, which was known across middle Tennessee as the absolute best anyone had ever eaten.

This side business for wild game processing had always been done in a separate area of the basement, to keep the meat from coming into contact with the products being sold to the public. Since selling wild game meat was illegal, they had never ventured down that path, although it would have been easy to do. Most of the hunters would throw in part of one the tenderloins as a "tip," or tell her to keep the stew meat, or a pack of steaks that didn't quite make the requested weight per pack of the customer. Consequently, Barbara had a large chest freezer full of venison, wild boar, a small turkey, along with slabs of bacon, ribs, odds and ends of beef chunks, and assorted other meat offerings when everything went down.

Business had not slowed down when the power went off. In fact, she was busier than she'd ever been. Folks had been coming to her with cows, goats, pigs, you name it, in any apparatus they could use to get it there. One guy carried a butchered goat across his shoulders while he rode a bike five miles to get to her. At first, she had no equipment she could use to process the meat. She could do it by hand, but it took a lot longer, especially when it came to the grinding. She was almost to the point that she was going to have to start turning folks away when Jasper showed up one day with a wild boar.

"Jasper, I'm sorry, but I don't think I can get this processed before the meat starts to go bad. I've got two deer, a pig, and a goat waiting already. Four critters a day is my absolute max capacity with no power."

Jasper looked dejected, then thoughtful, then brightened up. "How about if I could get you some power? Could you get me in then?"

Barbara crossed her arms with a huff. "Jasper Jenkins, just because you're an electrician does not mean you can magically create electricity any time you want to. Or are you saying you're an electrician magician?" She snickered at her own joke. Jasper Jenkins had served in Kuwait and Iraq during Desert Storm. He was retired from the Army, where he had trained as an electrician, an occupation he continued in after joining the private sector. As a master electrician, there wasn't much he didn't know when it came to dealing with electricity or electronics, to some degree.

Jasper cocked his head at her and smiled. "No, but I have a generator you can use, smart ass. I guess it's more important for you to be able to run your equipment than me to have lights. I was on city water so it wouldn't help with that anyway. I didn't have a lot of food at the house, just a bunch of microwave meals, which I went through pretty quick with the help of the genny. Being a bachelor has its downsides. You don't buy food for long term. You don't have things that make big meals if there's just one person. If you're dumb like me, you don't even have a bunch of bottled water stored up. I used to laugh at people who did that stuff, you know the 'preppers.' I guess they're laughing at us now."

"I doubt they're laughing, but I'm pretty sure they're telling all the naysayers '*Told ya so.*' I probably would be if it was me."

Jasper nodded in agreement. "Oh, I definitely would be. I'm just glad I had that salt water fish tank a few years ago. Got rid of the tank, but kept the five-gallon jugs I used to get the salt water in. I take those to the artesian well and fill them up. Twenty gallons lasts me a couple of weeks if I keep flushing to a minimum. This is one of those times when it's good to be a guy. The world is your urinal." Jasper laughed at his joke as Barbara shook her head.

"If all of you guys continue to pee wherever you want outside it will start to smell like it as well. I hope the mayor or the town council or somebody is thinking about things like this. Has anybody heard from any of them? It's been two weeks."

"Not that I know of, but then I've been kind of keeping to my-self. Without knowing how long this is going to last, you don't want people knowing what you have, no matter how little there is, you know? What if the power never comes back on? We don't know how big this thing is. No one from the government has been here, which makes me think it's the whole country. What are people going to do when the food runs out? How will they survive?"

Barbara replied, "Like the pioneers. Like the pilgrims. Like the forefathers. You grow your food or hunt your food. You make things or trade what you have to someone who does. You help your neighbor if they are willing to help themselves. You protect what's yours. People have been around a whole lot longer than electricity.

They did it. We can do it. You work or you die. That's how it was then, and that's how it will be now."

Jasper looked sad. "Well, I ain't a stranger to hard work, and I can hunt and fish so I won't starve. I might even be able to trade some meat for some vegetables. But I sure ain't looking forward to life without air conditioning. We might not die without it, but we may wish we had."

Barbara laughed at his comment. "Ain't that the damn truth."

****

Jasper had brought his generator to her, which made it possible for Barbara to run her freezer a couple of hours a day. With the modification to propane, she was not worried about her ability to keep things cold as long as she kept the freezer relatively full and limited opening it only during the times she had the generator running.

Her meat market had turned into more of a trading post. She had many different items that folks had traded her for meat. Everything from fresh fruits and vegetables to eggs and honey to clothing and shoes to guns and ammo could be found in her store now. All items were available to trade and many times she took the worse end of the deal to help people get what they needed or wanted. As long as she had food to eat and her roof didn't leak, she felt like she was doing okay, and better than a lot of others in town.

Since she was spending most of her time processing meat, she took on some helpers in the store. Jesse and Staci Hayes lived on the next street over when everything went down. They had no running water and very little food. Barbara invited them to move in with her. She had an old wellhead in the basement, from the early days before city water. The floor was concrete with a drain in the middle. A butcher has to have a way to hose everything off. Even after the city hooked them up, her father had kept the pump serviced and used it regularly for cleanup. He liked the feeling of pumping the handle and having water come out. He said it made him feel like a pioneer. Barbara was thankful for his pioneer spirit now.

Barbara had babysat Jesse when she was a teenager. He felt more like a little brother than a neighbor to her. They had three girls between the ages of four and ten, so they were extremely open to Barbara's offer of a job that paid in food and a house with running water—sort of. Jesse provided security and helped Staci with the store. Their oldest daughter, Alyssa, minded her sisters, Hailey and Jaclyn, in the apartment upstairs while their parents worked downstairs. She also took on an apprentice, as much to pass on her knowledge as to gain another set of hands. She chose a pair of hands attached to a strong young man named Eddie Brewer.

Eddie Brewer had been the biggest offensive lineman at the high school that anyone could remember. His parents were older than most of his friends' parents because Eddie was what is known as change of life baby—his mother got pregnant with him just as she was going into menopause. As they had no other children, the Brewers welcomed Eddie as a gift and doted on him. Now in their mid-sixties, with the health problems that come with aging, they were dependent on Eddie to provide whatever sustenance he could get since everything went down. Mr. Brewer had been a friend of Barbara's dad, so she had been trying to keep them in food quietly. If everyone knew how much she had frozen, she'd likely not be able to keep it. Eddie was very happy when she asked him to come work with her. Now he could provide for his parents and not feel like it was charity. For Barbara, it was more security. Not many people had the guts to challenge Eddie.

****

There had been run-ins early on with some of the folks in town. They seemed to be of the opinion that Barbara should just open the freezer and hand out all the food until it was gone. Doug Roberts had been one of the first to show up at her door, with a couple of friends, demanding she open up. He hammered the door with his fist, yelling toward her apartment.

"Manchin! Open up! We need the food you've got in there! We're in a state of emergency!"

Barbara opened the window from upstairs. "Excuse me? What the hell are you talking about? And stop beating on my door!"

He stepped back and looked up at her. "We need the food from your freezer. The grocery store is empty. Folks are out of food. We need your meat."

She stared at him in disbelief. "You seem to be confused. As you said, that is *my* meat, not yours, and not the town's. You are all more than welcome to buy some if you'd like to do business with me but it is not yours to take, nor demand that I give you."

Now it was his turn to stare, which quickly turned to anger. "What do you mean, buy? Money's no good, credit cards don't work. How are we supposed to buy it? We didn't buy the stuff at the grocery store. We just took it. First come, first serve."

"Yes, because when the power goes off stealing is suddenly legal, right? I heard what happened to Mr. Malone. He was beaten half to death trying to protect his store from looters. That won't happen here."

Doug was indignant. "We needed that food! We couldn't pay because, like I said, credit cards don't work and cash is no good. He didn't want to give it to us, so we took it. We didn't mean for him to get hurt, but he should have gotten out of the way. You should get out of the way, too, Manchin. We need that food you have, and

93

we're coming in to get it." He started to pull a gun from the waistband of his pants.

Barbara reached down and pulled up a shotgun, which she pointed in their direction. At the same time, Jesse opened the window beside her and did the same. Barbara gave him a smirk. "No, I don't think so. You're going to leave now, and if you come back, you'd best have something to pay with if you want meat."

Doug's face was fire engine red as he spluttered, "How the hell are we supposed to pay you? What do we pay with?"

"You got any more guns, or ammo? Hunting knives, sewing supplies?"

"Yeah, I got guns but if I give them to you, then I won't have any!"

She cocked her head as she considered his statement. "Can you eat them?"

He continued to fluster. "No, but … I can't give you all of it. I won't! What will you give me for … um, ten bullets?"

She shook her head. "Ten bullets won't even get you a half pound of stew meat. I'll tell you what. You come back tomorrow, with say twenty bullets, and I can sell you a quarter of a pound of chuck. But if you ever bang on my door like that again, or even think about demanding anything from me, I won't sell you one bite at any price. Now you go on home and see what else you might have that's worth a meal or two. I'm open to all reasonable trades.

You fellas have a good day now." With that, she closed the window. Jesse closed his as well, but he continued to watch the men until they left.

From that point forward, Jesse, Eddie, Barbara, and sometimes Jasper took turns standing watch in the store. Jasper brought in some sheet metal and fashioned doors with the help of Ben Vaughn. Ben was a ferrier and blacksmith by trade, but he happened to own a battery-powered welder that survived the pulse. No computer chips for the win. It took them a few days to get the doors ready and when they brought them out to install them some of the townsfolk stopped to watch. Doug was there and was vocal.

"What the hell, Jasper? What's going on?"

Jasper wiped the sweat from his brow. "What the hell does it look like, Doug? We're putting up some metal doors. You know, in case anyone gets any bright ideas about trying to loot this place like they did the grocery store."

Doug looked indignant. "What's that supposed to mean?"

"You know exactly what that means. Now, unless you mean to help, get out of my way so I can finish this job."

Doug stepped back and joined his buddies. They spoke low to each other then walked off. Barbara stepped in front of the doors. "Anyone who wants to buy from me can bring in whatever you have to trade. It can be other food, or ingredients; guns and ammo or knives; footwear or clothing in decent shape; sewing or yarn crafting supplies; sheets and blankets; anything that may be a value to someone else, or that another person might need. If you need something, come by and see if we have it. Everything we take in trade will be available to purchase in trade as well. Barter was around long before money, and it's a fair way to do business. Anyone caught stealing or trying to pass off something as their own that isn't, will not be allowed back. Y'all bring what you have to trade and we'll work something out." She turned to Jasper and Ben. "Thank you, guys, so much for this. Maybe we can all sleep at night again."

Ben smiled. "You're doing a good thing here, Barbara. Helping families by giving them jobs, giving folks a way to get food and supplies, and still pay in some way. I'm glad I could help."

Barbara waved a hand at him. "It's not like I could eat all that meat by myself, nor would I if others I cared about were hungry. This way, people are acting the way they should have been all along, instead of like criminals. There's no free rides, especially now. Everybody has to figure out how they can contribute to their community. This is my way."

"Don't sell yourself short. Not many people would care about others at a time like this. You've got a good heart."

She blushed, then said, "Aw shucks, thank you, kind sir. As soon as you finish that door, come inside for your payment. I've got a tasty venison tenderloin with your name on it. You too, Jasper, but you get bacon."

Jasper and Ben were both shaking their heads. Ben replied, "I didn't do this for payment, Barbara."

"I know. That's why I'm paying you. That, and this is how the barter system works. You provide a service, I pay you in goods. I won't take no for an answer." With that she turned on her heel and went back inside the store.

And that's how Manchin's Meats became Manchin's Trading Post.

Chapter 8

The first day the folks from town showed up to start planting was one we wouldn't forget. They arrived in a few old pickup trucks, beds full of people and gardening tools. Monroe, Jim, and Bob were on hand to help prepare the ground and had been working on it for a couple of hours already. Janet and I had a table set up in the shade with big coolers of water and cups. Ryan and Mike were there to watch everyone's backs. We hadn't seen any signs of the guys we now knew as Alan, Rich, and Steve, but that didn't mean they were gone. It just meant the sheriff hadn't found them yet. And neither had Mike or Ryan.

When the trucks pulled up, the guys went over to meet the folks from town. Monroe and Jim knew a few of them: Doc Hanson and Ben Vaughn, as well as Barbara Manchin. They all had services they could provide for their share of the crops, but they also wanted to contribute at the farm—at least until they got too busy with other things in town. Gary was making introductions when Clay came around the end of one of the trucks. Ryan immediately drew his sidearm and brought it to bear on Clay's head. One of the women screamed, then another, and suddenly everybody from town was running away from the scene, except Clay and Gary. Clay was standing wide-eyed, frozen in fear. Gary stepped between them calmly.

"Ryan, let's talk about this now. There's things you don't know about Clay. He's—"

Ryan didn't move, except for the hand holding the gun, which he moved to the side of Gary's head, holding the center of Clay's forehead in his sights. "I don't care, Sheriff. He was with them. He was one of them. He was part of the gang that killed my brother. It's my right to avenge his death."

Clay sputtered, "M-my brother got killed, too! We wasn't shootin' at n-nobody. We didn't even raise our g-guns. We was tryin' to keep from gettin' killed ourselves and Jay still got shot and died. Were you there? Did you see who did it? I'd like to talk to whoever that was, find out why they shot him."

Ryan let his pistol angle down slightly and looked hard at Clay. "That was your brother?"

Clay's lip trembled slightly. "Yeah. My momma took it real hard. I ain't lookin' for revenge or nothin'. I know we did it to ourselves. I'd just like to know why my brother got shot, of all the folks that was there."

Ryan let his pistol drop slowly until it was pointed to the ground but held Clay's gaze. "Because I was hurting. Because I needed to hurt someone else in my grief and rage. I didn't know who had been shooting, or who fired the shot that killed my

99

brother, Bill. I didn't care. I found a head attached to a body holding a gun and shot him. It just happened to be your brother." Ryan wasn't apologizing. He was calmly describing the events, like he might have been telling a customer they had moles in their yard and how to treat them in his former life as a landscaper. He did have a touch of something in his voice though. Not remorse, but maybe seeing it through Clay's eyes, at least from the standpoint of knowing the loss he felt.

Clay's jaw dropped. "It was you? You're the one?" Ryan gave him a curt nod. The anger flared in Clay's eyes, quickly replaced with regret. "I reckon I should be mad at you, but I ain't. Like I said, we shouldn't have been there. It was actually here," he waved his hand toward the burned-out house, "that we ran into those guys. We was tryin' to find more supplies, hopin' there was somethin' here. They showed up, cut the chain off the gate, and busted into the house. Then they made us go with them, over to y'all's place. We tried to stay back, but they threatened us, and our momma. We was just getting ready to hightail it outta there when Jay got shot. Guess we shoulda left about five minutes before that."

Ryan cocked his head to the side and gave Clay a grim smile. "Guess so."

Gary addressed Ryan. "Are you going to be good with Clay being here, working the gardens? This is his sentence for being there when it happened, whether he shot or not. He's paying his debt to society like the old working prisons used to do, with labor that benefits the group. We just don't lock him up at night. If it's going to be an issue, I can try to find some other way for him to do his penance but we really need all the able bodies we can get here."

Ryan looked from Gary to Clay, then back to Gary. "It'll be cool. He paid with his brother's life, too. Looks like we've got that in common now. But those others? They will pay, Sheriff. No second chances for those assholes."

Gary nodded and laid a hand on Ryan's shoulder. "Yes, they will, son. I'll make sure of it."

Ryan gazed back at Gary. "Then you better find them before I do. If I find them first, I'm ending them." He holstered his pistol and walked away to join Mike and the others.

Clay was visibly shaking. "Am I gonna be safe here, Sheriff? Is that guy gonna come after me?"

Gary shook his head. "You'll be fine. He's a good man and I trust him to do what he says he's going to do. Let's get over to the field and see what we need to do to help."

Janet and I watched the interaction along with everyone else there. The townsfolk seemed to have gotten over the sight of the pistol. Janet looked at me confused. "Why did they freak out, Anne? Isn't everybody armed these days?"

I looked around at the people milling about, some inspecting the work areas, others chatting amongst themselves. I saw a few sidearms, and a couple of rifles, even a few shotguns. But not even half the people had a weapon. Shrugging my shoulders, I replied, "Apparently not. I wonder how that's working for them."

At that moment, a young woman walked up to our table and asked for water for herself and her two small children. She stared at the pistols we had on our waists. I handed her the water, saw what she was looking at and smiled. "It's alright. I know how to use it. It's for protection from bad guys, nothing more."

She stared for a moment more, then said, "Can you help me get one?"

Taking a longer look at her, I saw an old bruise on her face, as well as the distinct imprint of fingertips on her arms. Not wanting to embarrass her, I continued to smile. "What's your name, honey? My name's Anne. This is my best friend, Janet."

Janet smiled at her as well. The woman gave a tight-lipped smile in return. "Kim. Kim Williams. These are my kids, Shelley and Shane."

The children hid behind their mother's legs. They looked to be between six and ten. They were dirty and looked half starved. My heart melted at the sight of them in need, then I put my shield up. *Don't do it, Anne. You can't save them all.* Yeah, I knew that, but it didn't make it suck any less.

Janet spoke to the children. "Well, hello there, Shelley and Shane. Say, would you like to come over here in the shade with me? If it's okay with your mom." She looked at Kim. Kim smiled a true smile and nodded. She took the children by the hand and led them away from the table. She nodded at me, her way of saying, "Now the grown-ups can talk."

I invited Kim to come around the table to sit in the chair Janet had vacated. She looked back at the fields, where people were planting. "Well, I really should be out there …"

I took her hand and led her to the seat. "You can go after we've had a chat. Oh, and we'll keep an eye on the little ones here in the shade."

She nodded and sat down. I sat beside her. "So, Kim, what happened? I can't help but notice the bruises. Did someone hurt you? Is that why you want help getting a gun? For protection?"

She looked down at her hands lying in her lap. I waited for her to answer on her own time line. I noticed as the tears started to fall but she never made a sound. Finally, she looked up at me.

"They came into my house. It was late. The kids were already in bed. I was lying in bed reading with a candle. It was so hot I just couldn't leave the windows closed. I was afraid we'd die from the heat. They just cut the screen in the kitchen and climbed through. I heard a noise and went to see what it was. They grabbed me. One slapped me hard in the face then clamped a hand over my mouth and pushed me to the floor. There were three of them. Two held me down while the other one …"

She stopped, the pain etched on her face. I was seething inside but I tried not to let it show. She took a deep breath and went on. "They saw the pictures on the wall of the kids. They threatened to kill me and do the same to them if I made any noise. So, I didn't. When the first one finished, they switched and another one started." She paused again. She seemed to be trying to stop the now uncontrollable sobbing. I waited patiently, hoping that the mask I tried to put on was in place, to cover the intense hatred of three men I didn't know but would gladly end if given the chance. After a moment, she gathered herself and continued. "When all three were done, they laughed at me lying there on the floor, naked and bleeding, walked out the front door, and drove away. I didn't get up for a while—I wanted to make sure they weren't coming back. When I did finally get up, I cleaned myself up as best I could with a few baby wipes, put some clothes on, went through the house and shut every window and door, and locked them. The kids don't understand why we can't keep them open at night. They're miserable, but I just can't take the chance … the chance they'll come back and do it again. Or worse, hurt my babies."

I tried to be strong, for this young woman I had just met, but I couldn't stop the tears from flowing, tears of anger and pain. Anger at the vile creatures who had done this to her. Even in my mind I couldn't refer to them as men, because that's not how a man is supposed to act. Pain felt in empathy for her from this ordeal. I took her hands in mine and, with tears shining in both our eyes, I finally spoke.

"Kim, honey, have you told anyone else about this?"

Her eyes grew wide. "Oh no, no I can't tell anyone. I'm so ashamed. If anyone else knew … I'm not even sure why I told you. Probably because I hoped you would help me if you knew why I wanted a gun."

While holding her hands, I felt her wedding ring. "What about your husband? Where is he?"

A fresh batch of tears started. "He worked the eleven to seven shift at a plant about thirty miles away. Because the work was so hot and dusty, he would take a shower before he came home, to save me the mess. He usually got out of there by about seven thirty. He never came home."

I nodded my understanding of a world where your car no longer ran and you had no supplies to sustain you on a thirty-mile walk, not to mention no means of protection. "So, you didn't have any guns in your home, I take it."

She shook her head. "I've always been afraid of them, and once we had the kids, I just couldn't stand the thought of having one in the house, even for protection like Boyd wanted. That's his name, Boyd. Oh, how I wish now I hadn't been so scared. If I'd had a gun when those assholes broke into my house … well, if I had one and knew how to use it. So, can you help me, Anne? Can you help me get a gun, and maybe learn how to use it?"

I had an idea already brewing in my mind, but I didn't want to say anything until I knew for sure it could be done. I squeezed her hands and said, "Let me see what I can do, Kim. I need your permission to tell the sheriff what happened. He needs to know that there are things going on in town like that. I believe we can get his help to get you what you want. To protect your family."

Wide-eyed again, she opened her mouth, I'm sure to beg me not to say anything, then stopped, closing her lips tightly. With a look of resolve, she gave me a curt nod. "Whatever we have to do, Anne. I don't want to be scared anymore."

I leaned over and hugged her tight. "Agreed."

****

I tracked the sheriff down and asked to speak to him.

He offered his hand. "Of course, Ms.—I'm sorry, I don't remember your name."

"Mathews. Anne Mathews. Please, call me Anne."

"Only if you'll call me Gary."

I smiled and nodded. I led him away from the crowd and quietly related the story of Kim's attack. I watched his face go through a series of changes: shock, anger, and concern among them. Then I shared my idea.

"Gary, we have firearms training every morning with our people. We want everyone to be able to use a gun if needed. Have you considered offering something like that in town? Do you have any idea who may or may not be able to defend themselves?" Now he had a new look on his face—embarrassment.

"I'm sorry to say I hadn't even thought about that, Anne. We've been so focused on getting food sources for everyone, security slipped by me. I wish Kim had come to me when it happened. We might have been able to catch them. I'll have one of my deputies set up a training schedule right away. Jasper Jenkins is retired Army. He seems to be a good choice for something like this."

I smiled and nodded. "Yes, our instructor is former Marines. That sounds perfect. The next question may be a more difficult request. How can we get the people armed? There aren't a lot of folks that are going to be willing to give up any firearms for something like this."

Gary looked thoughtful for a moment. "Well, there might not be a lot of folks out there who would donate, but we just happen to have some extras at the office. We'll try to figure out who is in the most need and see what we can do about getting them one. Kim will be at the top of the list."

We shook hands again. "Thank you so much, Gary. I think you may be surprised at how many people need and want the training. It will help you in the long run, too. The more people who can protect and defend themselves and their neighbors, the less ground you and your deputies have to cover. I'll let Kim know you'll be in touch."

I walked with a purpose to the field Kim was working in. No, we couldn't take everybody in, but we could do whatever was within our power to help them help themselves, if that's what they wanted to do. Kim wanted to protect her family. I was all in on that one.

****

Gary was surprised at the number of people who showed up on the square for firearms safety and defense sign-ups the next morning. Jasper wasn't.

"It's different for you, Gary. You wear the sheriff's badge and uniform shirt. Folks treat you better than others. I don't know whether it's respect for the office, or the knowledge you have a gun and know how to use it. Either way, your world is not the same one the rest of us are living in. I caught some asshole trying to climb in a window in the living room one night. Some bird shot in the general vicinity sent him running. I boarded up the window and started sleeping with one eye open. I can only imagine how it has been for others, especially the ones who never saw a need for a gun before."

Gary surveyed the crowd. There were men and women of all ages there, even some teenagers. He found Kim in the crowd and nodded in her direction. She smiled and returned the gesture. He turned to Jasper. "It would seem I have been lax in my duty to protect and serve. Security ranks right at the top of things you need in an emergency situation, but I was so focused on the food issue I didn't do anything about it. Let's fix that. Lord knows we need all the help we can get."

Gary looked out over the group. "Folks, thank you all for coming on such short notice. It has been brought to my attention that we've had some break-ins and attacks on our people. That stops now. If you have your own firearm and know how to use it, please step to the left. We can use your help with instruction, even if it's just how to properly clean a gun. If you are here to learn how to use one and don't have one of your own, step to the right. Also, if anyone has any firearms they would be willing to lend to a neighbor, please see me. Jasper, they're all yours."

Jasper stepped forward. "I'm going to need a few of you with experience to help with this training. Any volunteers?" Ben Vaughn raised his hand, as did Clint Russell. "Great. You two can start with the armed group. Check their weapons for maintenance and get a feel for their expertise with their guns. The rest of you, over here with me. We'll start at the beginning."

Gary had asked that they keep the training class to no more than an hour so the farm workers could go out to the gardens. Jasper used that hour to go over the basics of handling a gun—treat every gun as if it's loaded; know your target and what's behind it; keep your finger off the trigger until you're ready to shoot; don't point your gun at anything you don't intend to shoot; keep your weapon clean. The hour went by fast.

"I know we didn't get to do a lot today, but we need to get to the gardens. Classes will be every morning before the garden work. See you all bright and early!"

As the townspeople scattered to get to their appointed rendezvous point for a ride to the farm, Jasper, Gary, Clint, and Ben stepped off for a private chat. Jasper looked at his two co-instructors. "Well? What's the verdict? Clean guns?"

Ben was shaking his head. "Nah, most of them are hideous. I've got a few boxes of gun oil wipes I'll bring tomorrow, and some different sized bore snakes."

Jasper nodded. "I'll bring some, too. What about knowledge and skill?"

Clint snorted. "Some of them, yeah. A couple have had handgun training classes. A bunch of them were toting their daddy or granddaddy's rifle or shotgun that looked like they hadn't been cleaned since the original owner was alive. Them's the ones think they know cuz Grandpa let them shoot one time when they were twelve. When I ask somebody to show me their gun and they point it at me and say 'here ya go,' I don't have a lot of faith in their ability to use it."

"Who did that?" Jasper asked, the shock apparent in his voice.

"Doug Roberts. He's been prancin' around town with his daddy's old .357, barkin' out orders for people to donate their supplies to the town for everybody to use. He was at the front of that mob that robbed the grocery store. Thing is, there wasn't a community food bank set up yet, so reckon where all that food went? I'll tell you where—in their bellies!"

"I hate all that happened before I could get back," Gary said hotly. "It won't happen again—not that's there's any food left for them to loot."

"Oh, there's food, it just ain't unguarded." Jasper laughed. "He tried that crap on Barbara, and she pointed a shotgun at him. Told him to come back when he could pay."

Gary grinned. "God love her. I don't imagine he took that well."

"Nope and that's why me and Ben built them steel doors for her. Ain't nobody getting through those unless they have a tank."

"Well, here's hoping we can get people trained and armed so more of them can protect themselves and each other. I—make that we—just can't be everywhere. We need this for the town. Things have happened you guys don't know about, and I'm not at liberty to tell. Just know that, behind food, this is probably the most important thing we could be doing." Gary's impassioned statement had all of them nodding in agreement.

Jasper replied, "Don't you worry, Gary. We'll get them trained up."

Gary caught a glimpse of Kim loading herself and her kids into a pickup truck at the corner. He said, almost to himself, "The sooner the better."

****

Doc Hanson knocked loudly on the barred pharmacy door. "Brad? You in there? It's Doc."

Brad Wise came to the door. Doc heard the deadbolt lock turn then watched as the door swung into the darkened storefront. He heard the tinkling of the bell, one of many that had been above the door for thirty years or more. Brad smiled at his old friend.

"Morning, Doc! Let me just get that gate open." Brad unlocked the wrought iron gate and pushed it open. "Come in, come in. What can I do for you this morning?"

Doc walked through the door and shook Brad's proffered hand. "Gary stopped by yesterday and asked if you and I could get the clinic up and running again. Seems the folks that worked there never came back in after the power went off."

Brad closed the gate behind Doc, but left the door open. "I just opened the back door. Hopefully we can get a breeze in here. What can I do to help?"

"Well, I'm hoping you and my Hannah can create medicines we can use for the meds we no longer have. How is your inventory anyway?"

"I still have most of it. Dad had those iron gates installed on the front and back doors back during the late sixties, early seventies when the world was going crazy with war, segregation, you remember." Doc nodded. Brad went on. "We never had any trouble, and after a couple of years he didn't even bother locking them anymore. I did the same. Then the power went off. I didn't think anything of it at first. Strange for the power to go off when there wasn't a storm but who knows with all the parts that go into it. When I noticed nothing electrical at all was working, like phones and computers, I figured out pretty quick this wasn't just a blown transformer. I hightailed it down here with a shotgun and a pistol. Caught some bastards fixing to smash the front window with bricks. I fired my pistol over their heads and they took off. Been staying here ever since, with those gates locked. Had a few morons get the bright idea they could pull the gates off with a regular old pickup truck. I've dragged more than one bumper around back."

Doc laughed. "You said most. What happened to the rest?"

"Doled it out to folks who really needed it. The insulin is mostly gone, and I wouldn't trust what's left to work. Asthma inhalers, blood pressure medicine, blood thinners, those sorts of things have been picked up."

"Are you giving it away for free?"

"For the most part. I have a stack of IOUs from the ones who said they'll pay me when the lights come back on; not too sure when that will be. I've gotten food, bullets, silver, even a bit of gold as payment. I'll help folks as long as I can." Brad smiled. "Now, how can I help you with this request?"

Doc pointed to a walker with a seat built in. "Mind if I sit? These knees are giving me a fit today."

Brad wave a hand toward the apparatus. "Where are my manners? Of course, take a load off."

Doc eased into the seat and continued. "Ah, much better. I guess we—me, you, and Hannah—will work together to try to mend what we can and medicate if needed. I'd like to see us use natural herbal remedies wherever we can. Those will be around a lot longer than medications in case this lasts indefinitely. We won't be able to do anything about serious illnesses like cancer, or do open heart surgery or anything like that, but we can stitch wounds, set broken bones, maybe combat food poisoning. Hannah has a ton of herbs already dried at the house. Do you still grow them?"

"Some, but nothing on the scale Hannah does. So, what exactly would I be doing? Just dispensing meds here?"

Doc shook his head. "Oh, no, I want you at the clinic. You're a pretty good diagnostician. You can help triage the incoming patients."

"Well, I'm honored, Doc, but who's going to man the store here in case anybody needs anything?"

"We'll put the word out that we are on clinic duty in the mornings, and the pharmacy will be open in the afternoon," Doc replied. "If there's an emergency, folks will know where to find you. How does that sound?"

Brad smiled. "Sounds like a plan."

Doctor Albert Hanson, or Doc Hanson as he was called in town, had retired from his veterinary practice ten years earlier. At seventy-five, he had been enjoying a life of quiet just outside of town; that is, until the world turned upside down. Though his healing arts had been with animals, he knew the human anatomy well. He had served as midwife in more than one home birth when there wasn't time to get to a hospital. He'd stitched up his fair share of cuts. His wife, Hannah, was a naturalist, with a knowledge of herbs and folk remedies to rival anyone in the area, quite possibly the entire state. She grew many medicinal herbs in containers on her back patio. Their basement was full of dried herbs hanging in pretty much any previously empty space on the ceiling. People all over the county came to Hannah for her home remedies.

Brad Wise had been the pharmacist at the only drug store in town, Wise Drugs, for thirty years. His dad, Walter, had passed the store on to him when he retired, but Walt still went in almost every day to see his son and visit with the other "old folks" who came in to drink coffee and gossip about their neighbors until the day he died. The store was open every day from nine to six, except Sunday. It didn't really matter as everyone in town knew where Brad lived and knew his phone number. He answered it any time, day or night, and when the store was closed that phone forwarded to his cell phone.

When Gary pressed them into service, Doc wasn't sure he was up to it. His knees were about gone and he had been scheduled for knee replacement surgery two weeks after everything stopped working. He was resigned to the fact that he would probably use a cane, and possibly a walker for the foreseeable future. That's why the clinic would only be open four hours a day. Doc felt like that would be the max his knees could take.

The first week they were open, the waiting area was crammed with people. As it was officially summer, and there was no air conditioning, that made for smelly conditions and short tempers. Gary was on hand and put a stop to the riotous activity.

"Okay, everybody outside unless you are with the doc or one of his team. They're going to need room to work. Miss Hannah, I'm going to designate Jeremy here," he said, laying a hand on the shoulder of a teenage boy, "as your official gofer and name caller. Jeremy, I want you to help Mrs. Hanson with whatever she needs done, okay?"

Jeremy straightened up. "Yes sir, Sheriff. As long as she needs me. I've got some kind of rash Momma wanted me to get the doc to look at, nothing serious, just itchy. I can wait."

Hannah reached her hand out to Jeremy. "I think my assistant for the day can cut in line. Come with me, honey." She led him back to the room Doc was working in. She asked Brad if he'd take a look at Jeremy's arm. Brad looked at Doc. "You good here?"

Doc was examining a young woman who was complaining of abdominal pain. He replied while continuing to probe her abdomen, "Yeah, I think we have a case of not boiling our water before we drank it. Is that about right, Maria?"

She looked chastened. "I boiled it, but I guess it wasn't long enough."

Doc nodded. "Thought so. Go ahead, Brad. Hannah, I'm going to need a ginger tea recipe here, and some ginger. Maria, go with Hannah. Dear, you can send in the next patient." He wiped his brow with a damp handkerchief and took a moment to lean back against the wall on the stool he was using to give his knees a rest. Hannah peaked in before bringing the next person in and saw her husband leaned back with his eyes closed. She turned to the mother of two who were clinging to her legs and said quietly, "Give me just a moment, dear." She stepped into the room and gently closed the door. As she started across the floor, he heard her footsteps and opened his eyes. The concerned look on her face brought a smile to his.

"I'm fine, love, just needed a moment. Besides, we're almost done for the day. I can get through a few more."

"Alright, but I'm going to tell Gary that we can only see … what, three or four more?"

"How many are out there waiting?" he asked.

"Twenty at least."

He sighed. "Yeah, I can't get through that many. Have Brad go check them out and find the four who appear to need us the most. The rest will have to wait until tomorrow."

She nodded, kissed him lightly on top of his head and ushered in the mother and children.

Jeremy was dabbed with calamine lotion and given a small pill bottle of it and some cotton balls for later use. He was also given some allergy meds to take before bed. He stuck those in his pocket and helped Hannah by copying the ginger tea recipe to a few index cards. Brad went out to triage the crowd.

When they heard there would only be four more people seen today, the crowd got angry. Gary did, too—at the crowd.

"Hey! These people are doing this out of the goodness of their hearts! They aren't getting paid for their time or their supplies. Doc has bad knees and he can't stand for very long. We haven't had a clinic in weeks. I don't think one more day is going to kill anybody. Now the rest of y'all go on about your business and come back in the morning if you still need to see the doc."

They grumbled but dispersed, all but the four Brad had pulled out of the group. Brad looked at Gary. "Once we get through the initial rush of people who *think* they need to see a doctor, we'll be left with the people who really *do* need to see one. It'll quieten down."

Gary watched to make sure there was no trouble from the retreating crowd. "I'll be around just the same to make sure. We needed to do this, didn't we?"

"Yes, we did. Good thinking, Gary," Brad said. "We might even save a life."

Gary replied, "I hope you don't need to."

Doc walked out just then, leaning heavily on his cane. "Well, even without power to run tests or take x-rays, we managed to help some folks today. It'd be nice if we could at least get some lighting set up in there, but I reckon we'll get by—as long as my knees hold out. I had a couple of folks ask me about their livestock, wanting to know if they could bring them by. We may have to designate a day as critter doctoring day."

Gary grinned at him. "I'll get Jasper to come take a look and see what he can do about getting some lights hooked up for you. And you take your time, Doc. If it gets to be too much, stay home for a few days. The whole town is indebted to you, Miss Hannah, and Brad for this."

Doc shook his head. "No, this is our way of doing our part for the food that's being grown. No way I can work a field with these knees, though I could shell peas or shuck corn. Even that didn't seem like enough. Now, I know we're doing our fair share, and that works for me."

And that's how the Hanson Clinic got started.

Chapter 9

Lee put the finishing touches on the set of bunk beds he had built in the basement for the Scanlin girls. He stepped back, gave his work a critical eye and a satisfactory nod, then went upstairs and out the back door to get a breath of fresh air and check on his kids. He wasn't worried about them; they were with Sara, Marietta, and the rest of the kids for afternoon classes. He just liked to know where they were. Anything could happen in this world and, when it did, it was usually in the blink of an eye. Since the shootings, classes were held at the outdoor tables, which were close to the house, or in the screen porch if it was raining. It was a gorgeous, though slightly warm, day and the group of children and their teachers were at the tables which he had also built right after arriving at the farm. They still looked great, even after having weathered a few rainstorms. He was glad he had coated them with waterproofing sealant after construction.

As he watched Sara working with the children, he could see the pain and sadness she carried with her throughout every day. He knew that pain. He had felt that pain. Though he had resigned himself to the fact that his wife, Jackie, was lost to him, it didn't take the heartache away. He was finding himself less obsessed with what might have befallen her than at the beginning of this whole nightmare. He was able to remember good times spent with her and his family, which he tried to access whenever his mind wandered to the horrors she had probably faced. That was almost as hard as her being gone—not knowing what happened to her, if she was still alive, if she had been tortured or abused. He didn't have closure. He probably never would. Sara at least had gotten that.

She must have sensed him watching her because she looked up and gave him a small, sad smile. He smiled back and gave her a quick wave. Two people, from very different backgrounds, had found common ground in their grief. He walked over to listen in on the lesson. Though he tried not to distract the children, Moira saw him, waved, and yelled, "Hi Daddy!" She realized what she had done, disrupting the class, and slapped her hand over her mouth. The other kids giggled and snickered as she looked at Sara and sheepishly said, "Sorry, Miss Sara."

Sara attempted a stern school mistress expression, but quickly gave in to a giggle of her own. "That's alright, Moira. I think it's Daddy's fault more than yours for interrupting us anyway." She turned to Lee with a look of reproach.

Lee looked down at the ground. "Sorry, Miss Sara."

With that, Sara, Marietta, and all the children broke out in fits of giggles. Sara sighed. "Well, I guess class will be done early today as I doubt I will ever get you all to concentrate now. Please go see if

Miss Millie or one of the other moms needs any help. If not, you are free to play until supper."

A round of whoops and hollers ensued as they rushed to the back door to see if there were chores to do. Sara and Marietta gathered their meager school supplies. Lee moved in to help. "I really am sorry, Sara. I didn't mean to disrupt your class. I just wondered what y'all were working on."

Still smiling, she replied, "No need to apologize, Lee. We were working on some math and spelling. I'm not sure how far we are going to be able to go academically without books or supplies like pencils, pens, paper, those sorts of things. We have some supplies, and they will probably last a few months, but once they're gone …" She trailed off and didn't finish the sentence.

Lee nodded in understanding. "Yeah, Anne has said something about that, too. She made a great suggestion. If we could get our hands on some chalkboard paint, we could make slates out of wood. I can smooth out some fencing slats and cut them down to size. We'll figure something out."

Sara looked thoughtful. "I wonder if there is a school close by. If there was, maybe we could venture out to it, see if there were schoolbooks, chalk, possibly that paint—I wonder if we could get that excursion approved."

"I doubt it, but there's no harm in asking. Let's go find Russ and Mike."

"Wonderful. Let me just help Marietta finish gathering the children's things and I'll be ready."

Marietta shook her head and waved them off. "Go ahead. I've got this. It won't take a second to finish."

Sara laid a hand on Marietta's arm. "Thank you, dear. Cross your fingers we get a yes."

Marietta held up both hands with her fingers crossed. "Times two!"

Sara laughed and walked toward the house with Lee. As they went, Lee replied, "We better cross everything we've got to get a yes for this one."

****

"No. Absolutely not." Russ had barely heard Sara's proposal before he shot them down.

Lee said in a frustrated tone, "Now wait a minute, Russ. At least hear her out."

Russ was shaking his head. "That is not a critical list of items needed for our survival."

Sara put her hands on her hips. "It may not be necessary for our survival now, but do we never look past that? There has to be more to this new life than just *surviving*, Russ. Even the pioneers had books and slates to teach their children how to read, write, do arithmetic. Surely that need has not disappeared with the lights. They still need to learn these things. Moira is six now. If this lasts for ten years, would you want her to be sixteen with a first-grade education, facing whatever our lives have become by then? How would she survive in that world? I beg you to reconsider."

Lee looked at her with a modicum of pride, Russ with surprise etched on his face. He pondered for a moment, then said, "Wow, Sara, I don't guess I had thought about it that way before now. Of course, I don't want Moira, or any of our children for that matter, to be any less capable of dealing with the future we have waiting. I'm just not sure what it will take to make this happen." He looked to Monroe. "Monroe, is there a school close by? Maybe more than one?"

"Not so close you could walk to it," Monroe said. "You'll have to take a truck or something. All three schools are close to town, about six or seven miles away, and they're all right next to each other. Maybe we could talk to Gary the next time he's out to Jim's place. He should be back today or tomorrow for sure. Tell him what we need, see if he'll at least check to see if the stuff is there before you make the trip."

Mike replied, "That would be my choice for how to proceed. But, what about this chalkboard paint? I've never even heard of it before. Where would we get that?"

Russ answered him. "Chalkboard paint is kind of a new thing. Turns pretty much any surface into a chalkboard. You could get it from craft stores. The sheriff might know where we could find that, too. There's no telling what's left in town now, but it doesn't cost anything to ask." He turned back to Sara. "I'm sorry I was so quick to say no, Sara. It's easy to forget that, even during the apocalypse, there's more to life than food, water, shelter, and clothes. We'll do what we can to fulfill your request. If you could put together a list of everything—"

"I just happen to have one right here," she said, as she pulled a piece of paper out of her back pocket and held it out to him. Lee turned to hide a smirk, while Russ laughed and took the proffered piece of paper.

"Okay, we'll talk to Sheriff Burns as soon as we can. Consider your request a go, unless we say otherwise after we see him."

She turned to Lee with a huge grin and held her hand up to him. He gave it a slap and her a laugh. "Way to plead your case. Good job, Miss Sara."

She blushed. "Thank you, Mr. Lee." She inclined her head toward the back door. He gave a short nod and headed that way with her.

After they had left the house, Mike spoke quietly to Russ. "Is there something … I mean, are they …"

Russ watched them go out, then turned to Mike and shrugged his shoulders. "I don't know, buddy. A bit soon for her, I'd say, but they do have common ground. It wouldn't surprise me if they go down that path. If there's anybody here who knows what she's going through, it's Lee. Frankly, I think it'd be good for both of them."

Monroe snorted and pushed his way between them. "Y'all gossipin' like a couple of ole biddies. C'mon, let's go see if Gary is at Jim's."

Russ rolled his eyes while Mike hid a laugh behind a cough. He grabbed his rifle and headed for the screen door. "Sure thing, Monroe. Lead the way."

****

"How are you doing, Sara? How's Tony doing?" Lee glanced at her as he asked, then looked back in the direction they were walking, though they hadn't discussed a destination or plan of action. The afternoon was warm but, beneath the boughs of the huge trees in the yard, the breeze made it a bit more comfortable.

She sighed softly. "I guess as well as one could expect in this situation. I miss him terribly. I cry myself to sleep at night. Kate gave me something called valerian root to help me sleep. It's supposed to have a calming effect. It smells like feet and tastes like it smells." She paused as Lee snorted a laugh. "I'm not kidding. It tastes awful. However, it does seem to help. At least I can sleep a few hours a night— after the gag reflex has calmed down." They continued their stroll through the yard, each in their own thoughts, at least for a moment. "Do you still mourn for Jackie, Lee? I'm sorry—that's a stupid question. Of course you do—I know you do. I see it in your eyes. A sadness that your smile never quite gets past."

He stopped and turned to her. "Damn, I thought I was doing a better job of hiding it than that, for my kids' sake at least. And yes, I still hurt. The ache has dulled somewhat but it's always there, just under the surface. I still wonder what happened to her, still have nightmares thinking about the horrors she might have faced ... probably faced. After what happened here ... oh shit, sorry. And sorry for my potty mouth ..." Lee was blushing with embarrassment.

Sara giggled. "I was married to a trucker, Lee. I've heard worse."

Lee grinned at her. "Yeah, I bet you have. So, how did you two meet?"

They spent the next hour or so wandering the yard, finding out more about each other, though it seemed like only minutes to them. When Janet leaned out the door to announce that supper was ready, Sara jumped with a start. "My goodness, I had no idea it was this late. Where has the time gone?"

Lee looked at the house then back to Sara. "Thank you for a wonderful afternoon, Sara. I feel like you and I are a couple of lost souls walking the same path. I hope we can talk more another time. It felt kind of therapeutic, you know?"

She smiled and replied, "Yes! That's exactly how I felt. Like you are one of the few people here who can understand what I'm feeling, what I'm going through. Yes, we'll definitely talk again, soon. I have to run. I hope the ladies don't think I was trying to get out of food prep duty, although most of them are much better cooks than I am. I'm learning a lot from them."

"I'm sure they handled it fine. You know what they say about too many cooks in the kitchen."

"You're so right, and if they put me in charge, I would definitely spoil the soup."

They both laughed as they headed toward the house, Lee calling for his children to join them. They all walked in the front door together, looking very much like a family.

****

Russ, Mike, and Monroe caught up with Gary at the Dotson farm. There was a lot of activity. Matt Thompson was running the tractor, discing up nice, neat rows for planting. Ryan was on guard duty, at his request, and was watching in all directions with binoculars from the roof of a truck that had been used to bring the townspeople out to plant the fields. The owner, Silas Jones, stood beside it glaring up at Ryan. Finally, in an exasperated sounding tone, he barked out, "Hey fella! This truck is an antique and in mint condition! I spent a lot of money getting it restored, and now it's worth even more than it was before, since it's one of the few running vehicles in town. Do ya mind getting off the roof before you scratch the paint up there?"

Ryan looked down at the man. "Yeah, I do mind. I'm only up here watching for the kind of people who would love nothing more than to take this antique, mint condition truck from you. I don't see a gun on you. Do you have one?"

"No, I don't. Why would I? I've never needed one, and never wanted one. So what? What does that have to do with your stomping around on the roof of my truck?"

Ryan jumped down into the bed, then out to the ground next to Silas. Mike and Russ had been watching the interaction, along with Gary, who started over toward the men. Mike held his arm in front of the sheriff. "Hang on. Let's see what happens. I don't think Ryan will do anything rash."

Gary stopped, but continued to pay close attention to the two men. "I hope not. We don't want any trouble. We've had enough of that."

Ryan looked Silas in the eye. "Uh, what's your name?"

"Silas Jones. I own—"

"Yeah, I don't care. Look, Silas, in case you haven't figured it out yet, pretty *things* are no longer important. Surviving is. This truck is now a survival tool. It serves whatever purpose needed to help you survive. Being pretty is not necessary. Now, if it's okay with you, I'm going to get back up there and make sure no assholes get the drop on us and try to take your pretty truck. Does that work for you?"

Silas stood there looking dumbfounded. When he didn't respond, Ryan jumped back into the bed of the pickup, then climbed back on the roof.

Russ and Mike looked at each and laughed. "I think I just saw a bit of the old Ryan, Mike. What do you think?"

Mike replied, "I think you're right, Russ. I missed that little smart ass."

Russ turned from Mike back to where Ryan diligently stood his watch and said with a smile, "Me too, buddy. Me too."

****

Armed with Sara's list, Gary and Tim went to the schools. The windows in the doors had been broken in and the doors were left standing open. Gary shook his head. "There are some folks in this town who really need …"

Tim finished his sentence. "A good ass whuppin'. Yeah, Doug comes to mind. Asshole. Guarantee him and his buddies did this, looking for food."

Gary stepped through the broken glass into the darkened interior of the elementary school and turned his flashlight on. "Yes, and I'm sure they took all they could find. There would have been bulk cans of food in the storerooms. Let's go check."

They made their way to the cafeteria. As they got close, they heard a scuffling sound coming from the kitchen. Both men stopped to listen, then drew their pistols. Walking slowly, they advanced toward the noise. Gary rounded the corner of the storeroom. His flashlight pierced the darkness and lit up two sets of eyes. The raccoons squawked at them and scurried out the other door. Gary chuckled nervously. "Too bad we didn't have a shotgun with us. I hear they're decent eating."

As they walked into the storage room, they could see that it had been ransacked, and not by the four-legged critters. The raccoons had been eating cracker crumbs from the floor, which was pretty much all that was left. Every shelf was bare. Gary fumed.

"Those selfish pigs! You know they didn't share one bit of what they took from here with anyone! If they took everything from all three schools, there's no way they've eaten all that. I want to find their stash, Tim. Fast. It could help the folks in town now. First, we check for the school supplies since we're here."

They entered the first classroom they came to. It looked to be about third grade level from the posters on the walls. Multiplication tables, cursive writing, and a map of the world were prominent.

"Well, I figure we should start here, since these kids would be learning the basics, and should have been using basic supplies. We can't take everything, but let's get some samples to take back. If Russ and his people want to come get more, they can. Lord knows other people have helped themselves to supplies here. At least these folks are trying to do something good with them."

They gathered pens and pencils, writing tablets and paper, some schoolbooks, and chalk and erasers from the chalkboard rail. Looking in the teacher's locker, Gary pulled out a can of paint. Chalkboard paint. "Well, I'll be damned. Look what I found! That paint they were talking about that turns anything into a chalkboard. Wonder what the teacher used it for?"

"I'd say these." Tim pointed to the cubbies the children used for backpacks, lunchboxes, winter wear, or any other personal items. Each one had a small piece of wood attached to it that had been covered with the paint. The child's name was written on the surface. Plastic wrap was laid over it and secured with tape to keep the name from coming off. "Pretty smart. Each year, they just take off the plastic, put the new kid's name on and wrap it back up. Recycling at its best."

Gary added the paint to his own backpack. "Man, that teacher out there is gonna be tickled to get this. Let's check the other two schools. Textbooks shouldn't be a problem for the kids. Maybe we should find out how many teachers we have that are still around.

Once the crops are done, we need to keep the kids occupied so they don't get into trouble. Idle hands and all that."

Tim nodded. "Agreed. I think we'll have plenty enough to keep us busy without a bunch of kids getting into or causing trouble. I'll see what I can find out in the next couple of days."

Gary patted Tim on the shoulder. "Thank you, Tim. I really appreciate how you've stepped up in this crisis. Now, let's go check out the other two schools."

****

Sara was ecstatic over the supplies Gary brought them. "Oh, Sheriff, this is amazing! And you say there's more?"

Gary smiled and nodded. "Yes, ma'am, quite a bit more. I'd ask that you take only what you absolutely need for the kids here though. We're going to find other teachers in town, see about getting a similar setup there this fall after the crops are in. Probably in the library, so we can have them all together in one spot in the center of town. Like the old one-room school houses, all grades, all together. Should be interesting."

Sara laughed. "Yes, it should. Children today are not as, shall we say, well mannered, as children back then were. Perhaps good behavior will make a comeback since there aren't as many distractions for them."

"Let's hope. I need to get over to the farm and pick up a load of folks to take back to town. Y'all have a good evening." Gary got in his truck and drove off.

Lee took the can of paint and looked it over. "Guess I've got some work to do. How many slates do you need?"

Sara considered his question. "Can we make a dozen? And if there's any left after that, I'd love to have a large chalkboard to use."

Lee replied, "Hmm. I don't think there's that much in here, but maybe we can get one from one of the schools when we go for more supplies. They usually have some on rollers to use in the auditorium. That would probably be better."

"Oh yes! That would be perfect! I'm so excited—it's like Christmas in June! Wait, is it still June?"

Lee looked to be working out the date in his head. When he did, he had a shocked expression on his face. "Holy shit! It's Independence Day!"

****

We were all blown away when we found out what the date was. How could we have let that sneak up on us? But, when you didn't have a "job" to go to, the days kind of ran together. The chores were the same every day. Life was pretty much the same day in and day out. This Fourth of July would not be celebrated as it had in the past, though. No burgers and dogs on the grill; we didn't have the meat or the buns. No potato salad or pasta salad; we didn't have mayo for the dressing. I never figured out a way to keep it long term, and it doesn't last outside of the fridge. We had already planned chicken and rice for dinner that night which was pretty much done, so to celebrate Millie baked a batch of cupcakes. She even tinted the frosting with strips of red, white, and blue. Even though it was steamy, the guys built a bonfire. We sat back away from it because it was July after all, but it was pretty. Sean brought out a fresh batch of moonshine and poured drinks for the grown-ups. The kids got apple juice in a plastic highball glass. Russ stood and raised his glass.

"I'd like to propose a toast. To everyone here who have all worked so hard to help get the place to where it is. To everyone out there, trying to make it without hurting other people. To those we have lost," he said, moving his glass toward Sara and Ryan, "and those still here. On this day when we celebrate our hard-fought independence which was won at great cost to our countrymen and forefathers, may we always remember that freedom isn't free, and the fight for our freedom never ends. There will always be others who want what we have, or just want to see us fall. Whoever put us in this position wants to break us, to have us fighting each other so that they can come in and scoop up whatever and whoever is left. We won't give up and we won't give in. We are not quitters. We are Americans! Cheers!"

We all responded in kind, then sipped our drinks. The moonshine was amazingly smooth and burned all the way down, just as I expected it to. I closed my eyes as it slid down my throat to my stomach then immediately made a U-turn back up to my brain. I'm not going to say I was a lightweight, but we hadn't done much drinking since we moved to the farm. Most of us were so worn out from the day's work that we went comatose at night, no nightcaps needed. That was great, just to be sitting by the fire, enjoying a drink, like our world wasn't turned upside down. It rocked.

Chapter 10

The next morning, Carrie leaned out the back door and spied Ryan walking from the bunkhouse toward the gate. He'd just come off security detail, but was going back for more apparently. "Hey Ryan, can you give me a hand in here?"

Ryan stopped and turned toward her. "Sure, Carrie. What do you need?"

She smiled at him and held the screen door open, inviting him in. "Just a little muscle. We're trying to get everything rearranged in the clinic downstairs since Lee finished the bunk beds. It's going to open up some more room for us and Kate wants to use every available space we can. I think she's afraid Anne will commandeer some of it for other supplies if it looks unused."

From the kitchen, I yelled, "I heard that! And she's probably right!"

Carrie giggled, which elicited a grin from Ryan. Looking through the window above the sink at him, I swore I almost saw our old Ryan in his face. Interesting. He walked to the screen door, pushed it open, and inclined his head for her to precede him. The gentleman move. Very interesting. He gave me a nod as they headed for the basement. I smiled back and watched as they went through the doorway that led to the stairs. Was this a budding romance in the making? Oh my goodness, that would be so good for Ryan. Something to move him from the dark past into a bright future. I threw up a quick prayer that just that would happen.

As they went down the stairs, I heard them talking. Not that I was eavesdropping, but the world was a whole lot quieter now and sound of any kind carried very well. Carrie asked him what his plans were for the rest of the day. Ryan replied, "I was just gonna head back out front, help out with the watch. Why?"

"Well, I was thinking if you could get the afternoon off, we could go look for some elderberries. There are some bushes back behind the campers a little way that I think might be them, and I know I can't go by myself, so I was wondering if you'd come with me. Miss Millie said there were some back there at one time, but that it had been years since she went out that way. They are great for flu symptoms and can ease the pain of sinus infections, sciatica, nerve pain and such. They also boost the immune system so with a lack of doctors, and some day, multivitamins, I figure we can stock up if we have some close by, maybe make up some tonics and tinctures, or dry some for teas. We just need to find them first."

"Do you know what they look like? Or are we just gonna go breaking off limbs and bring them back here for Miss Millie or someone to identify?" He took on a teasing tone with her, another shadow of the old Ryan.

"Yes, smartass. I mean, I've never seen one, but I have this." I peeked around the corner to see what she was showing him. She held up the mini tablet, with the color photos of plants. Man, was I glad I had loaded the survival, prepping, and homesteading books on that, too! A black and white e-reader was nothing compared to a color photo when you were identifying a plant. Go me!

He grinned at her then. "Gotta love Anne's gadgets in the apocalypse. Sure, I'll escort you on your plant-finding adventure. When do you want to go?"

"Right after we finish filling up this space so it looks like we're actively using it. You know, because Anne ..."

"I can hear you down there!" I had gone back to the sink where I had been washing up some ginger I had pulled from a plant in the "farmacy." We had been inundated with the occasional upset stomach in the past week or so, and were hoping it wasn't an issue with the water supply or some kind of bug. With our folks working over at the Dotson place and being around the folks from town, they could very easily bring some kind of crud home. Ginger is well known for its ability to ease stomach issues (ever had your mom give you ginger ale when you were nauseated?), so I was helping Kate and Carrie out with getting some chopped up for teas. "I have no idea why you all think I want all the extra space around here.

Tell me one thing I have put in a place that wasn't designated for it."

They had come back up the stairs by then, and Ryan looked at me with a smirk. "How about the bucket tower in the bunkhouse? You took the whole corner up with stacks of buckets of beans and rice and I don't know what all. We were planning to put a dartboard on that wall, if we could find one. Bill and I—" He stopped at the utterance of his brother's name, that had rolled so easily off his tongue, as the raw pain of that loss seemed to envelop him. He stood there with his eyes closed, took a deep breath, and continued. "We had one at our house on a wall that would have needed a lot of patching if we had ever decided to sell the place. Bill was great at darts, I wasn't half bad, but we had some buddies who really sucked at it—especially after about a dozen beers." He appeared to have pushed the hurt back inside, and even graced us with a small smile.

We had completely run out of room in the root cellar after the Dotsons got there and added Charlotte's home canned goods to the mix. The food in the buckets was at least inside mylar bags with oxygen absorbers, so they could handle probably six months to a year without a loss of nutritional value in what would become higher temps in the bunkhouse with no air conditioning. Trying to get our happier Ryan back, I ribbed him again. "What's more important: a dartboard or food? Can you eat a dartboard?"

"No, but I could eat *off* a dartboard; you know, like a platter." He grinned then, and there was our Ryan for another moment. "Aren't you the one that likes things to have multiple uses?"

I laughed out loud at that, something we hadn't heard or done a lot of in the past couple of weeks. "Carrie's right—you are a smartass. Go find her plants."

They headed for the door and Ryan placed his hand on her back as he held the door for her. Definitely something brewing there. I smiled at the thought. Carrie could be the very thing to bring him back.

I jumped a foot when Millie spoke up behind me. "Yes, I do believe there might be something wonderful happening between those two young people."

"Geez, Millie, you scared the crap out of me! And, yes, I agree, and it makes me very, very happy at the thought."

She grinned at me, then went to watch them walk across the yard to the fence row. "I was afraid we might have lost him to the pain he's kept inside. It happens that way a lot. The ones who are the most outgoing, the most gregarious, are the ones who hold their emotions deepest. They let the world see the face they want it to see. The darker parts they hide away."

I was watching them through the window as well. "I know he has so much love to give. You can feel it when he smiles at you, or hugs you because you gave him a fresh cup of coffee. Or at least you could, before …"

She turned from the door and joined me at the sink. "You're right, and I know for a fact the love of a good woman can turn a man around; it can help him break down the walls he builds to keep the world away from his heart. I have a feeling we'll see our former Ryan again. Maybe not entirely the same, but a more mature version who is ready to start a new chapter in his life. Ready to love someone more than he loves himself. Now, what can I do to help get the ginger ready? I heard one of the Scanlin girls, Katlyn I believe, saying her stomach was hurting."

"If you insist, you can put some water on to boil in the kettle. We'll make up some ginger tea, a big batch. I think a couple of the other kids are complaining with the same thing. Lord, I hope we don't have a bug starting."

"Well, dear, if we do, you can pretty much count on a bunch of people getting it. We are living in pretty close quarters." Millie filled the kettle from the pump on the sink.

I sighed. "No matter how much you preach to wash your hands and be careful around each other, it happens, especially with this many folks. I'll get some honey to put in the tea as well. That should improve the taste, and the tummies."

With the soothing properties of the ginger and the antimicrobial properties of the honey, we were truly hoping to nip whatever this was in the bud and quickly. We didn't have time to be sick. Summer was here and the real work was coming.

****

We were getting into the summer months and the gardens were coming on fast. We had fresh fruit and veggies at every meal. We were canning and drying every day trying to keep up and not lose anything. Fortunately, we had three experienced hardcore canners in Millie, Charlotte, and Casey. They had pots going inside and out just about non-stop during daylight hours. We also had food and herbs in the drying racks Millie had shown us how to use. During one particular canning session, pickles were the focus. Pickles are a good source of antioxidants and aid in the supply of probiotics, which help with food digestion. Now you know why that garlic dill pickle was served with your sandwich at the deli. The cucumbers were almost out of control so we were doing our best to get the most of them. Still, we had some that had sat for a few days before we could get them canned. Casey questioned the more senior ladies as to the viability of the cukes as pickles.

"I'm not sure these can be saved," Casey said, shaking her head. "The skins are turning white already. They will probably be mushy. Yes, that's the voice of experience talking. I lost a half-dozen jars that way once."

Millie smiled at her. "Well, let's see if we can give them a little help. Janet, go outside and grab some leaves off those grapevines back by the fence."

Janet looked quizzically at her aunt, but did as she asked. I looked at Millie and started to ask what was up, why the grape leaves, but she silenced me with a raised finger. "Just wait. When Janet gets back, I'll share with everyone." Spooky how she could tell what you were thinking half the time.

Janet came back in with a handful of the leaves and asked the burning question we all wanted answered. "Why do you want these leaves, Aunt Millie? What do they have to do with making pickles?"

Millie took the leaves to the pump on the sink and rinsed them off. She handed them to Casey. "Put half a leaf in each jar before you process them. Grape leaves are naturally rich in tannin, an enzyme that promotes crispness without adding alum to the process for pickles. My grandma taught me that a long, long time ago." Did I tell you that woman was a wealth of information?

Casey did as Millie instructed and the pickles were put in a water bath canner outside. Ten minutes to process, then about a week until the taste test. When the pickling spices were gone, we had plants that could contribute to our lifestyle without actually being food. And once again, the old ways were becoming the new ways.

Jim Dotson added even more knowledge of primitive food preservation by showing us how to make jerky without a dehydrator or oven. Hunting had been successful in the woods around us. We didn't have a lot of folks out there competing with us for the game—yet. Ryan hadn't been hunting since the loss of his brother but Jim and Carrie had, as well as Bob and Lee, who were hunters in training. They were good for a couple of rabbits, a few squirrels and a deer or wild turkey almost every day. The smaller critters were incorporated into the day's meals. The larger were either canned, smoked, or dried. We made a lot of deer jerky.

The setup was basically a three-pole tepee with no cover. He then tied sticks between the poles to drape the meat over, which had the added benefit of giving the rustic structure more stability. The drying setup was out in the open where the sun was on the meat most of the day. The kids helped him set it up, then were given the responsibility to keep the bugs off. Tony was in charge of keeping a small fire under it, barely burning with green wood so it smoked a lot, which created a natural bug deterrent. The younger kids took turns keeping an eye out for any stubborn bugs that weren't deterred, and were equipped with hand fans to run them off. Once the meat was completely dried, it was loaded into jars or zipper bags and added to the dry stores.

Since the episode with the marauders, we hadn't been as diligent about daytime fires as before. The bad guys (that we knew about) knew where we were so we didn't think there was a need to try to hide it. Also, the folks from town who were working the community gardens knew we were in the area. But then again, we had beefed up our security since the incident. We had two more on watch with the previous four. One patrolled the house, yard, and

145

trailer areas, another the field behind the trailers. The meat drying we needed to do during the day when the sun was out so we had no choice but to have the fires. As well, the natural predators of the night wouldn't be so apt to try to obtain the food during the day.

Jim had spotted some coyotes behind the campers during a particular jerky making session. He said they seemed to be less afraid than they should have been with that many people out and about. Perhaps we were putting a dent in their food supply with the increase in hunting in the area. Tony began carrying a twenty-two rifle slung over his shoulder while we were drying meat, joining the ranks of the rest of us toting rifles. No sense taking chances with children out and about.

We talked about the people in town. We had to give them credit— they stuck it out and stuck together, somewhat, from what Sheriff Burns had told us. They had a chance of getting through this if that attitude continued. Still, there would be people who didn't want to have to sweat in a garden all day to grow food. Too many days at a desk and nights as a TV zombie, when all you had to do was slap a frozen dinner in the microwave or order a pizza and have it delivered, had made most people soft. An hour workout at the gym is nothing like spending four to six hours in the hot sun, because you don't plant crops in the shade; bending over, squatting down, pulling weeds, or chopping them with a hoe, all while dealing with flies, mosquitoes, gnats, and ants; with sweat running down your face, burning your eyes; perspiring so much that every stitch of your clothing is stuck to you, embedded with dirt from the dust you've raised tending the crops. Couple that with the knowledge that you won't be able to take a nice hot, or even lukewarm, shower when you're done because you have to use the water hauled there in fifty-five-gallon drums to water the crops if it hasn't rained—and no one had a working shower anyway. With the exception of a couple of the older folks, no one had any idea what they were going to have to do to create food for themselves and their families. They had no concept of how hard it can be to grow things without the modern machinery used by huge farms before the pulse to grow millions of pounds of food, or the ability to produce water on demand from a hose or sprinkler system. To keep a daily vigil over the precious plants for pests that would try to steal them for themselves, including the four-legged and the two-legged kind.

The hardest part was the waiting—waiting for the produce to mature so it could be consumed. The lettuces and radishes had broken ground and were taking on the look of actual food. Beans and cucumber plants were growing as well. A lot of precious gas has been used to till up lawns in town, but the skeptical now saw the value. They had food growing right outside their doors. Which of course presented another problem: those folks that didn't want to do the work for their food. There was a mysterious rash of garden theft from folks who didn't have fenced yards. Seems the thieves weren't hungry enough to climb fences—yet. Or perhaps they were just taking the easy way. It seemed like it always came back to there being some who worked for what they had and others who wanted to live by taking what someone else had.

****

From what Gary had shared, they had set up a community larder at town hall. About a half dozen men and women hunted daily, donating all but about 25 percent of their kills to the food bank. For their donations, they were given fresh vegetables like leafy greens in the beginning. As the summer wore on, a portion of the vegetables would be eaten when harvested, while the majority of the food would be canned for the winter.

They had established basic medical services, for both human and livestock. They had a leatherworker who was using the hides from the animals taken for food to make shoe soles, scabbards for knives, and rifle slings, among other things. They had a butcher who had taken on two helpers to process the meat, both wild and domestic. He said she had a large freezer being run by a system that utilized a spiral wind turbine to generate electricity. That was impressive to those without power. Setting up the solar power system at the farm never seemed to get moved up the line in front of food and security. Mike was very interested in the turbine setup though, and wanted to go into town to see it. Monroe said he'd go along as well, and Bob and Brian rounded out their group. They took Bob's SUV so everyone could fit comfortably. Mike instructed

Matt to get the pole put back in front of the gate after they were out and leave it up until they got back.

When they arrived in town, the guys were impressed with the changes they saw. Many houses had nice little gardens where landscaped lawns once grew. Most people were out in their yards, either tending their garden plots or sitting in the shade of portable canopies. Even in the heat of a Tennessee summer day, some shade outside was better than the heat of a house with no air conditioning or working ceiling fans; houses that had not been built in a manner that would let a breeze blow through.

Monroe took in the scene as they drove slowly down main street, waving at the people he knew. "See? This is what life was like before television. People didn't hole up inside the house all day. It was too damn hot. When they finished working their garden they'd sit on the porch, or in the shade of a tree and try to cool off. The houses were built with windows on all sides so you could get a cross breeze blowing through them when the womenfolk were cooking in the kitchen, but it was still cooler outside. Folks had big porches on their house and they'd sit out there until dark, or longer if they could stand the skeeters. They weren't sitting on the couch staring at a machine talking to them. They talked to each other. I think we was better off back then."

Bob nodded as he drove. "Can't say you're wrong about that, Monroe. But I do miss that air conditioning."

Mike and Brian laughed from the back seat. They pulled up in front of the meat market and climbed out of the car. Barbara met them at the door, wiping her brow with a towel.

"Monroe! So good to see you. How's Miss Millie doing? Glad you folks are making it through this apocalypse okay. Come inside, although it may be cooler out here. This heat is really getting serious."

Monroe smiled and walked over to where Barbara stood, now wiping her blood-stained hands on the towel. He shook her hand, then introduced the men with him. "We come to see your electric setup, Barbara. Mike here has some electrical expertise and wanted to see how you all got this turbine thing going. Mind if we take a look around?"

"Absolutely not. The turbine is on the roof. There's a stairway out back that will take you up there. Come inside after you get done and see what we've done with the place."

They headed out back and Mike and Brian went to the stairs. Bob stayed behind with Monroe. Mike looked at him over his shoulder, "Still afraid of heights, Pinky?"

Monroe cackled and Brian hid a smirk. Bob glared at Mike. "Shut yer pie hole, Sergeant."

Mike laughed and climbed the stairs to the roof above the second floor. They found a unique looking turbine and Mike's eyes lit up.

"This is what I was talking about right after we got to the farm! I saw this online before everything went down. It's supposed to be super efficient at generating wind power."

Rather than your standard windmill, Jasper had, with the help of Ben Vaughn, created a huge metal spiral, cone shaped, with cross bracing to hold the form. It made almost no sound. Brian grinned at Mike's enthusiasm.

"This is a pretty sweet setup. I wonder how much power it generates."

"Let's go down and ask," Mike replied excitedly. They hurried back to the stairs and rushed down.

Mike looked at Monroe and Bob with a huge grin. "Man, that thing is great! Let's go talk to Barbara and see how it performs. I bet we have the materials at the farm to make something like it."

Bob looked sideways at Monroe. "I don't doubt that one bit."

Monroe replied, "Shut yer pie hole, Pinky!" Everyone but Bob was rolling with laughter.

They walked into the shop and looked around. As Monroe was the only one who had ever been there before, his eyes got big as he took it all in. Shelves lined with canned goods, both factory and home canned, though more of the latter; stacks of material, as well as spools of thread; baskets of onions; flats of eggs; used clothing, footwear, and tools. There was chopped firewood lining the entire wall under the shelves.

"You've been busy, Barbara. Got yerself a nice little trading post here. You turnin' a profit?"

Barbara laughed. "I have no idea but I doubt it. We trade meat for whatever they bring in that might have a value to someone else. If someone needs something we've got, they trade something else for it. I have turned down a few that brought in power tools and electronic devices. Not really a lot of call for those these days. I figure I'm usually on the losing side of the deal, but at least people are trying to do it the right way."

Bob picked up a pair of high-heeled sandals and held them aloft. "Probably not many fancy dances to wear these to either."

She grinned. "No, but that gal was completely clueless as to how to feed her kids with no grocery store. I told Staci here to go ahead and make the trade. Do y'all know the Hayes family?"

She introduced Staci and Jesse, as well as Eddie. Mike was walking around the store and peered into what used to be a meat display case. It now held long guns and ammo. Most of the guns were older, possibly belonged to someone's grandparents at one time, and the ammo was mostly in small bins of loose cartridges. He looked at Barbara. "Got yourself a collection of antiques too, I see."

She nodded. "Yes, we don't get a whole lot of guns, since those now have multiple uses—security and food acquisition. I do get the occasional old single shot rifle as you can see. I also have a few handguns, but I keep those locked in the safe. Too easy to pick up and pocket when someone's back is turned. Been there, done that. If y'all need anything though, I'd be more than happy to bring them out."

Mike shook his head. "Unless you've got an automatic rifle hidden somewhere, I think we're good. I would like to know how the turbine setup is performing for you though."

Barbara smiled again. "It's great. I can run the freezer most of the time. Just to be on the safe side, I try to run it four hours on, two off, and only open it during the power on times. I spread the word through town that barter times are eight to twelve in the morning and two to six in the evening. Whoever is on sentry duty each night manages the two to six on and off cycle. So far, so good. Come on down and check it out."

They all went down to the basement. The fact that it was noticeably cooler down there wasn't missed by anyone. The Hayes girls were playing there and stopped to stare at the newcomers. Bob greeted them.

"Well hello, ladies. Is that a tea party I see? I sure could use some nice cold tea on a hot day like this."

Alyssa jumped up, grabbed a teacup, and hurried over to Bob with it. "Would you like lemon in your tea, sir?"

He took his pretend sip. "Ahhh. No, ma'am, this is perfect just like it is. Thank you kindly, little lady."

She giggled and ran back to her sisters. Barbara walked over to the walk-in freezer. "They play down here during the heat of the day. It's way too hot upstairs in the apartment."

Monroe looked around at the evidence of people living there, not just visiting. "They staying here with you then?"

Barbara nodded. "It's easier to cook for a few than one. Plus, Jesse helps with security, so he's on watch every third night in the store. It just made sense to bring them here for the duration."

"Pretty much what we did on the farm, just on a bigger scale. We've got about two dozen folks out at our place."

Barbara's eyes grew wide. "Wow, that's a bunch of folks. I'd heard you had a little community out there. Good for you, Monroe. We need to take care of each other, and watch other's backs now."

Monroe replied, "Yep, at least the ones who are willing to do their part and help the group, not just take what someone else worked for."

"Thus, the reason for the security." She told them about the run in with Doug early on, demanding she give them what she had in her freezer. "Had I done that, given them everything, this place wouldn't have become what it is, which is an asset to the community. Most people are happy to part with something in payment for a product. There's pride in knowing you can do that. Plus, it's kind of become a meeting place for folks, so I get all the info about what's going on in town. I'm not in this to make a profit now, obviously, but I'm happy to provide a service."

154

"You're a good woman, Barbara. Your daddy would be proud of ya." Monroe paid the compliment sincerely.

"Thank you, kind sir. I sure hope so." They walked back up to the storefront.

Just then Jasper walked in. "Monroe! How you doin'? I've been meaning to come out to your place and see if you've got some parts I'm looking for. I finally rounded up enough to get Barbara's freezer going but I could use a few things like inverters, capacitors, you know electrical components that weren't plugged into anything when the pulse hit. You got any stuff like that?"

Monroe shook Jasper's hand and inclined his head toward Mike. "Talk to our resident creator here. Mike, this is Jasper Jenkins. Fellow Army grunt and licensed electrician. Jasper, this here is Mike Thomas. Former jarhead. If you can think it up, he can pretty much figure out how to make it and make it work."

The two men shook hands. Mike said, "We do have some of those items, but we'd like to use a lot of them to set up some power resources ourselves. I'm really interested in how you built that turbine on the roof. I can't get over how quiet it is. Do you have a schematic, or a drawing of it?"

"Nah, me and Ben just kind of hammered it out—literally. Ben's a blacksmith. I told him what I wanted, he took some sheet metal and formed it. We mounted it and almost immediately it started spinning. The rest was hooking up the electrical components. The sheriff wants one for his place, the sheriff's office. He and his wife, the mayor, fixed up the basement of the office there and are living in town. I wouldn't mind having one at my house, truth be told. At least I could have lights and fans then, cuz damn it's hot."

There was a group acknowledgment of the heat statement. Bob replied, "Yep, summer in Tennessee is pretty rough without a/c. What do you think, Monroe? Should he come out and see what goodies you've packed away for a rainy day?"

"Yeah, I reckon that'd be alright. We don't let just anybody on the place, Jasper, but I'm sure you ain't lookin' to see what you can get your hands on—other than them electrical things."

"That'd be great. Can I come out later today? Or tomorrow?"

Monroe nodded as he headed for the door. "Either one's fine. Now, if you fellas are done jawin', we need to get back home. Good to see you, Barbara. Take care now. Keep up the good work."

She waved. "You, too, Monroe. Tell Millie I said hi!"

"Will do."

"I'm gonna try to come out there this afternoon then, Monroe." Jasper was walking with them to the SUV.

"Alright. I'll tell the fellas on guard duty to keep an eye out for ya."

Jasper looked at him quizzically. "Guard duty? You got guards? Have you had trouble? Oh wait, I heard about those guys attacking your people. I'm real sorry about that, Monroe. Seems there's more and more bad elements cropping up now."

Monroe stopped and turned to Jasper. "I don't think we've seen the worst of it yet. The longer this goes on, the more desperate folks will be. It's going to get real ugly. You shouldn't be living at home by yourself, Jasper. You need folks to watch your back."

"Well, Barbara has offered more than once to put me a cot in a corner of the basement. Said I could help with security to pay my room and board. Maybe I should take her up on that."

"Yes, you should. We'll see ya later this afternoon. I hope you remember where the place is, cuz you probably won't find it if you don't."

Jasper looked at him in confusion again. Monroe laughed. "You'll see."

****

Jasper understood Monroe's comment when he got to the driveway—or at least, where there used to be a driveway. It was grown up pretty good, though there were distinct tire tracks where the guys had driven out and back in earlier. He pulled up and parked, got out, and walked to the gate, which just looked like brush at first glance.

"Hello! Jasper Jenkins here. Monroe said I should come out and take a look at some parts."

He watched as the gate opened, marveling at how well hidden it was. Mike greeted him with a smile.

"Hey, Jasper. Glad you could make it. Please drive in. We don't want your truck sitting out on the road broadcasting the entrance."

"Sure thing. Be right in."

Jasper drove through and the gate was closed behind him. Matt and Nick came out of the foxholes and waved. He stopped and Mike climbed in the cab.

"Just head on up to the house. We've got all the electronic components boxed up in the barn."

"Wow, y'all got quite the setup here. Security, camouflage, everything. This your doing?"

"Some, but the gate was done when I got here. They did some planning for something like what happened."

"I'll say. I had no idea Monroe had changed the place so much. When did they do all this? I know it's been a few years since I was out here, but that's a lot of growth out front."

"I think they did it all over the last three or four years. Just pull up over there by the barn."

They got out of the truck and walked up to the barn doors. Monroe was there, as well as Bob.

"Glad you found the place, Jasper," Monroe said with a grin. "What'd ya think about our modifications?"

"Impressive as hell, Monroe. What made you think to do all that before anything even happened? Mike said you worked on it for a few years."

He turned to Bob. "This 'un here and his neighbors. They're preppers and they planned for the farm to be their bug out location."

"Bug out location? Did y'all start your own army?" Jasper asked, clearly confused again.

Monroe laughed. "No, but we do have a few folks here now. That's the term preppers use for leaving their home if there's a catastrophe of some kind and it ain't safe to stay. You know, like if all the electricity is gone and who knows when or if it's coming back."

"Well, that was some good luck for you all then. So, you had food and gas and stuff stored up?"

Monroe grew quiet. "We did, but I'd appreciate it if you didn't spread that around. Pretty sure we ain't seen the last of all the assholes running around trying to take other people's stuff yet."

"Hell no we ain't. There's some in town stealing right outta folks' gardens, right outside their doors!"

"Yeah, we heard about that. Any idea who it might be?"

Jasper replied, "Gary's got his eye on a couple of guys that ain't working in the community garden, ain't hunting, and don't have their own garden, but don't seem to be losing any weight, if you know what I mean."

"I surely do. Them's the ones you gotta watch out for. They'd rather take than work."

They had been walking toward the plastic bins that held the electrical components as they talked. Mike opened one of the totes to reveal inverters, controllers, meters, and other assorted parts. Jasper's eyes grew wide.

"This stuff still works? All of it?"

Bob beamed. "Sure does. Our Faraday cages protected everything in them. What are you in the market for, sir? We'd like to do some bartering."

Jasper looked inside and started picking up different items. "I don't have much to trade. I gave Barbara most of what I had that was worth anything to get her system up so her freezer could work. I could probably get you fellas a deer in the next day or so, if that would work."

Mike smiled at him. "You have something better than things. You have knowledge and experience. I'm passable with electrical setups, but nothing compared to a master electrician. We want your help setting up a solar and wind turbine system here. If we can get some power, it sure would help to have our freezer and refrigerator running, as well as some ceiling fans and lights. Think we can get enough power for those things?"

"As long as you don't try running the water heater and air conditioning, or the well pump, you should be able to generate enough power for the rest. Those 220-volt appliances eat up the power. Things with heating elements are tough, too."

"Anne won't be happy about that. She's been nagging us almost daily about hot, running water in the house," Bob replied.

Jasper nodded. "Yeah, the womenfolk are right fond of that one. Unfortunately, that takes more juice than most everything else you named put together. My suggestion is try to get the most bang for your buck. Maybe she'll be happy having the fans running instead."

"I don't guess she'll have much choice. Have you met Anne? She doesn't take no well. I don't want to be the one to tell her. You tell her, Mike."

"Pass."

"Chicken."

"Pot or kettle, Pinky?"

Jasper looked like he'd been left out of an inside joke as the rest of the men shared a laugh. He shrugged his shoulders and said, "Okay, how about we set aside what we know we'll need for the set up here, and then I can have a look at what's left?"

Monroe grinned. "Sounds like a plan."

Chapter 11

Doug had been quite busy in the early days after the pulse. He scavenged all the empty houses around his and quickly realized the food he had found and taken wouldn't last him long. He started trying to think of places where he could get large amounts of food. The group he had joined to loot the grocery store had talked about banding together to pool resources but many were distrustful of each other and it ended in a fight. Everyone grabbed as much as they could, fighting over a few items like chili and soup, and took off. Since then, Doug had been working alone gathering resources until he remembered the schools. He ventured out one night, breaking into the elementary school first. He hit the jackpot. Cases of institution sized number ten cans of vegetables, meats, even pudding filled the larder off the kitchen.

"Ho-lee shit!" he exclaimed out loud. "I found the mother lode!" The problem was he had ridden a bike there, since his car was too new and no longer ran. *How am I gonna get this to the house?* He quickly ran through the list of people he would be willing to share this haul with who still had a working vehicle, even though he didn't want to share any of it. He knew he would have to so that whoever he chose would agree to haul the stuff back to his house. He just had to figure out who he could trust to keep their mouth shut about it. He settled on Kevin.

Kevin Barnes had been a buddy of his since high school. They hung out a lot when they were teenagers. They weren't as close now but Kevin had been in the group that looted the grocery store so chances were pretty good he'd be up for this. Not wanting to take the chance that someone else thought of the cafeterias at the school before he could get them cleaned out, he went straight to Kevin's house.

The place was dark but he thought he saw the glimmer of a lamp or candle behind the blinds. He knew Kevin would be armed, so he knocked on the front door and called out at the same time.

"Kevin! You in there? It's Doug. I need to talk to you."

The door opened just far enough for one eye to peer out at him. When he saw that it was indeed Doug, he opened it a bit wider. "What the hell are you doing here this time of night? What do you want?" He didn't invite Doug in.

"I've found a shit ton of food and I need someone to haul it. I'll split it with you—say, seventy-thirty. All you have to do is haul it back to my house, then take your share and bring it back here."

Kevin eyed him suspiciously. "Where is this stash?"

Doug shook his head. "Not telling unless you agree to the deal. Are you in?"

Kevin opened the door wider. "Sure, if I get the seventy. My truck, my gas."

Doug's mouth dropped open. No way! Fine, I'll go sixty-forty then. I get the sixty."

Now Kevin was shaking his head. "Not gonna happen. Tell you what. I'm in if we go fifty-fifty. Your find, my truck, your muscle, my gas. That's fair."

Doug scowled at him for a moment. Finally, he said, "Fine, fine! But we gotta go now, before someone else finds it."

Kevin returned the scowl. "It's fucking dark! Why can't we do it in the morning?"

"Because this can't wait that long. I ain't stupid but I ain't a rocket scientist either. If I could think of this so could someone else. We need to get the stuff now."

"Shit. Alright, c'mon in while I find my shoes. In the dark."

Doug stepped through the doorway. "Okay, just hurry the hell up. We don't want to lose this one."

****

Kevin whistled when he saw the food. "Oh man, you weren't lyin'. This is a gold mine! What made you think of it?"

Doug was shining his flashlight over the food stores. "Just trying to think of places that stored a lot of food for a lot of people that weren't actual stores. I came up with schools and prisons. Prisons might have people still in them but schools? No way. Let's get busy. I haven't even checked the other two yet."

They loaded all the food from all three schools into Kevin's truck. It took them the better part of the night and multiple trips but they cleaned them all out. Doug stored his part in his basement. It took him days to get it all down there since Kevin told him his duty ended at the garage. At first he was pissed, then he thought, *What else am I gonna do? It's not like I gotta go to work.* He chuckled at the thought.

When he had finished, he had number ten cans stacked floor to ceiling along an entire wall two rows deep, plus a pile of fifty-pound bags of flour, sugar, cornmeal, and instant milk. To celebrate, he opened a big can of fruit cocktail. He sat in the floor of the basement eating his fill and estimating how long he could live off the food he had now. *I bet it's years.*

****

Gary went to Doug's house right after he left Manchin's. He had stopped to pick up Jasper on the way for backup. He was relatively sure Doug was the culprit who had cleaned out all three school cafeterias, but he had to see for himself. He told Jasper to wait in the truck and walked up the front steps. He knocked on the door and called out, "Doug, you home? It's Gary Burns."

Doug peered out through the curtains. He yelled back from inside the house, "Yeah, I'm here. What cha need, Sheriff?"

Gary looked to the windows and saw Doug. "I'd like to talk to you. Could you come to the door please?"

Doug hesitated, then walked to the front door. He opened it but left the security chain in place. "Okay, I'm here. What's up?"

Gary looked frustrated. "I'd like to talk to you about some town resources that have gone missing. Can I come in?"

"You got a warrant?"

"Do I need one?"

Doug seemed to consider that, then closed the door, slid the chain and opened the door wide. "Naw, I got nothing to hide. C'mon in, Sheriff."

Gary walked through the doorway looking around. As with many single men during the apocalypse, house cleaning was not an important trait or a priority. There were clothes and dirty dishes laying all over the living room and kitchen, which he could see from the door. The house smelled of unwashed clothes, stale beer, possibly urine, definitely body odor. The room was stifling, with the windows shut and the curtains drawn. Gary wrinkled his nose. "You know, you might want to open some windows, air this place out a bit. How can you stand this heat?"

Doug looked around the room. "I guess I got used to it. I sit out back in the shade a good bit. So, what's this all about, Sheriff? Whatever resources you're looking for, they ain't here."

Gary was still surveying the rooms. He didn't see any evidence of the missing food stores, but he also couldn't see the whole house. He turned to Doug. "Someone broke into all three schools and cleaned out the cafeteria storage. I'm looking for that food. It would help the townspeople greatly and, by all rights, it belongs to everyone. Do you know anything about it, the missing food?"

Doug shrugged his shoulders. "Nope, I don't know anything about that. Is that it?"

Gary looked him in the eye. "Mind if I have a look around then?"

"Yeah, actually, I do mind. You got a warrant? This is still America last time I checked."

Gary narrowed his eyes. "No, I don't have a warrant, but I can get one in about ten minutes. And I can wait here while I do. Is that the route you want to go down?"

Doug's eyes darted left to right, as if trying to find an escape. There was none. With a heavy sigh he replied, "Okay, fine. Yes, I have the food from the schools—well, half of it. It's in my base-ment. But, it was fair game, Sheriff. I thought of it, I found it. Why shouldn't I get it?"

"You broke into the schools to get it. That food was paid for by the people of this town, all of them. They all have a right to it. Just because you got it, doesn't make it yours. What if someone broke into your house while you were out and took it. Would that be fair game, since you weren't home?"

"Hell no! That's different. This is my home. I own it and everything in it."

Gary nodded. "Exactly. The people, the citizens, the town owns the schools. You stole from everyone in town. I should arrest you for grand theft."

Now Doug looked scared. "But, but, I wasn't looking at it like that! I was scavenging empty places, just like everybody else. Why am I in trouble and nobody else is?"

With a disgusted look, Gary said, "Because you took enough food to have easily tided the town over until the crops came in. Because while you were sitting here with a full stomach, women and children in town were starving. There's no excuse for that level of selfishness. Now, where's the food?"

Dejectedly, Doug replied, "In the basement. I'll show you."

"No, I can find my way. I need you to go outside. My deputy will be with you while I take a look."

Gary walked him to the door and motioned to Jasper to join them. When Jasper got there, he asked, "Any luck?"

Gary nodded. "Seems so. I'm going to take a look. Keep Doug company while I do."

"Sure thing, Gary."

Gary turned and went back in the house. He found the door to the basement and went down. When he saw all of the food cans, he was livid. "Selfish bastard," he said aloud. He stormed up the steps, through the house, out the door, and straight to Doug. Grabbing him by the shirt front, he said through gritted teeth, "You said you had half. Where's the other half? Where's the rest of the damn food?"

"K-k-k-Kevin has it! Kevin Barnes! I swear, Sheriff!"

Still holding Doug by his shirt, Gary looked at Jasper. "There's so much food down there. We could feed the town for a month, easy. If there's twice as much, we can get through the next couple of months, maybe more. I need you to stay here and guard this place. I'm taking this piece of shit to the jail for now, and picking Tim up to back me up at the Barnes's place. We'll be back with able bodies and vehicles to haul this stuff in. We'll need to set up guard duty for the food at the community center when we get it back. This will definitely be worth someone trying to take. I'll be back as soon as I can. You got water?"

Jasper gave him a quick nod. "Yep, I'm covered. Do what you gotta do."

Gary let go of Doug, spun him around, and yanked his hands behind his back. After slapping a set of cuffs on him he pushed him toward the truck. "Get your ass in that truck. If you try anything—anything at all—I'll shoot you. Do you understand me, you selfish prick?"

Doug stumbled, catching himself before he fell. He righted himself and turned to Gary, eyes full of hate. "Yeah, I understand. Just remember, *Sheriff*, when you're threatening people like that—every dog has his day."

"That wasn't a threat. It was a promise."

****

Doug went to Kevin's door with Tim at his side. There was no wondering this time. He knew Kevin had the food. When Kevin saw through the peephole that it was the sheriff, he opened the front door. Gary pushed past him and walked into the house.

"Hey, what's going on here? You can't just barge into my house like this!" Kevin said indignantly.

Gary replied, "Actually, we can. We have reason to believe that you are in possession of stolen goods." He was scanning the room as he said it. Among the trash and dirty clothes, he spied a couple of large cans sitting on the floor, empty. He gave Kevin his full attention. "And the evidence is there," he said, pointing to the cans.

Kevin crossed his arms over his chest. "That don't mean nothin'. How do you know I didn't have that from before?"

Gary looked at him, disgust written all over his face. "Because the packaging is different for bulk bought by institutions. It's very generic … like those."

"Maybe I bought bulk online."

Gary shook his head. "Kevin, you know damn good and well you stole that and a whole lot more. We already have Doug in custody. He gave you up. Stop lying to me."

"That little piece of shit. I shoulda known he'd cave at the first sign of trouble. Fine, yeah, I've got the food. Well, half of it."

"Where is it?"

"Back bedroom. I'll show you."

Gary shook his head. "No, you stay here with Tim. I can find my way."

Kevin jerked his head toward the hall. "Last room on the left. I've got a lot of stuff in there that is legitimately mine. It best all be there after you take the food."

Gary stopped and turned back to Kevin. "So, it's okay for you to steal from others but not okay for them to steal from you. Is that what you're telling me?"

"It wasn't stealing! It was scavenging! Everybody is doing it."

Gary took a couple of steps back into the living room. "Let me see if I can explain the difference to you. Scavenging is going to the house of a person who has died, or just didn't make it home when everything went down. Getting a few days, maybe a week's worth

171

of food and supplies. Stealing is taking things from people who are still around, like the whole damn town."

"How is it taking from the whole town? Everybody ain't got kids in school. That food was bought for the school kids."

"Right. Who are still here. And starving, by the way." Gary shook his head. "You and Doug are cut from the same bolt of cloth. All you see is what's in it for you. You think you're entitled to all that food back there while other people in town—who, for your information, paid for that with their tax dollars—suffer. I've seen you at the meetings we've held, discussing how to move forward. I saw you with your hand out taking some of the rations we dispensed. I'm pretty sure you were part of the looting party that emptied the grocery store and almost killed a man. All the while, you were sitting on enough food to feed them all. You disgust me."

Kevin stopped him. "Now wait right there, Sheriff. We didn't have this food when we cleaned out the grocery store." Realizing he had just admitted to what Gary already thought to be true, he said, "I mean …"

Gary held his hand up. "Stop before you admit to any other crimes, Kevin. Just sit down over there and keep your mouth shut."

Gary walked back to the bedroom and did indeed find the rest of the food stores. He also found guns, ammo, jugs of water, and smaller piles of canned goods; kerosene heaters and lanterns; stacks of blankets, clothes and footwear. He went back to the living room.

"Well, it looks like you've done quite a bit of scavenging. Also looks like you've thought ahead to winter. Heaters and blankets—why?"

Kevin looked at him grim faced. "Hell, you know as well as I do this ain't no ordinary power outage. This is bad, and it ain't gonna get better for a long time. Everybody is thinking about right now, sweatin' their asses off. What about six months from now? What they gonna do when there's no heat? Them fancy gas logs ain't gonna do shit, are they? No, we're way more likely to freeze to death than burn up."

Gary cocked his head and considered what Kevin had said. "Kerosene heaters don't work without fuel. Did you think about that?"

Kevin snorted. "I ain't stupid, Sheriff. I've got fuel. I just ain't got it in the house. It's out back in the garage."

"And where did you get that?" Gary asked.

"I already had it! I keep kerosene on hand all the time. It don't go bad like gas, and it works in heaters, lanterns, even refillable lighters."

Gary nodded. "Okay, I'll give you credit for doing that. I can honestly say it's more preparing than I had done." He looked at Tim. "We need to load all this food up and get it town. It's going to take more than my truck. Jasper has a trailer we can use. We can probably do it in two loads, one from each place, with that and a truck. I'm going to take him to jail. I'll pick up Jasper's trailer and get back here as quick as I can. I'll grab a couple of guys in town to help. We should be able to get it all loaded and back to town before dark."

Tim asked, "How come we aren't making him and Doug help? They stole it. They should help get it back."

Gary replied, "Because I don't want to waste space in the truck with their asses. I'll bring a two-wheeler to hopefully help get it out and loaded quicker. Oh, and tarps. I don't want the folks in town knowing about all this until we have it secured."

"Why's that, Sheriff?" Kevin asked.

"Because hungry people are desperate people. I don't want anybody to die over some cans of food they should have had access to all along. I want to make sure we have it in a place we can control and use it for the good of everyone. Everyone." He pointedly glared at Kevin when he said the last word.

"So, how come you get the say so over it? How come you get to divvy it out? Who made you boss of the town?" Kevin retorted.

Gary gave him a grim smile. "You did. You and everybody in the county did … when you elected me sheriff."

"Not me," Kevin stated with a smirk. "I voted for the other guy."

The supplies were taken to the community center and a guard duty was set up to protect it. Angie was ecstatic when she heard about it.

Good news travels fast, and before long, the street out front was filled with people from town with questions as to the distribution of the food. They were becoming increasingly louder and more agitated. Angie and Gary decided they needed to get them focused on how the items could best be used. Gary stepped out on the landing and held his hands up. "Folks, can I have your attention please?" He waited and there was no decrease in the volume of voices. He spoke louder. "Folks! I need you to quieten down and listen!" There was a slight lessening of sound but not quiet. Angie put her two index fingers in her mouth and let out a shrill whistle. Everyone looked up then. She turned to Gary with a smile, and saw he was chuckling to himself. He leaned over and whispered, "Thank you, darlin'." She nodded and looked at the crowd. Gary began.

"I'm sure you've all heard about the cache of food we got from the schools."

"We heard Doug and Kevin took it, then you took it from them." Silas was of course the first to interrupt. "Thanks, Sheriff. Now when do we get some of it?"

Gary held one hand up. "Please, let me finish. I don't know how many of you have ever bought or used industrial sized cans of food. There's about two dozen servings in one can, depending on the contents. If we start handing out cans, some of the contents could go bad before it gets eaten. Also, do you want a large can of green beans, while your neighbor gets a large can of corn, and the next person gets a large can of tomato soup? I think we should try to get the most out of this in a way that benefits everyone."

Loretta King raised her hand. "What if we set up a soup line, Sheriff? We could make soups or stews, those take a few cans of ingredients put together to make big pots of food. Did you get flour or cornmeal?"

Gary smiled at the intelligent woman. "Yes, ma'am, we sure did, and instant milk, too. You reckon you could whip up some biscuits or cornbread to go with that soup, make it go a bit farther?"

She grinned and nodded. "I reckon we could do that. There's a big kitchen in there with the pots and pans we need to cook that big. I can't do it by myself, mind you, but I can surely take charge of it if I can get some helpers."

Gary mouthed, "Thank you" to her and surveyed the crowd. "That sounds like a great plan to me. Who would like to volunteer to help Miss Loretta? This will be an everyday thing, people. Don't offer if you aren't willing to be here when she needs you. We'll also need people to cut and haul wood for cook fires for them."

Dozens of hands raised, both men and women. "I'll help." "Me, too." "Count me in, Sheriff."

Gary said, "That's great. Everyone who wants to volunteer, see me after this meeting. We'll get started first thing in the morning."

Silas whined, "But what about tonight? What about now? We're barely getting enough to survive and all that food is in there …"

Gary rolled his eyes. "Silas, you are not going to shrivel up and blow away before tomorrow. Go home, go to bed, and try not to think about food. You'll make it. We are not going to waste a bite of this food. Now everyone who isn't volunteering can go on home. Come by in the morning for an update."

There was some grumbling, but most of the people disbursed. The volunteers stayed and talked to Loretta, Gary, and Angie. A plan was made to start early the next morning on their first meal.

There were a few hiccups at the beginning. Estimating how much they needed to make to feed all the people took some practice. They didn't have ovens to bake bread in, so they started with a collection of Dutch ovens and skillets, cooking over an open fire. One of the men in town saw the dilemma and built them a large cob oven. They only served one meal a day in the late afternoon, so they had plenty of time to bake bread all day for them to have enough for the meal. Some of the fresh produce was used for the meal but anything that could be canned was done while the cooking was going on. The hunters brought in game for the meat used in the soups and stews. On Sundays, there was some type of cobbler or sheet cake if they could get their hands on some eggs. Loretta was in the middle of it, and seemed much younger than her eighty years. The townspeople were getting one good meal a day. With the gardens still young, that was more than Gary and Angie could have hoped for. Life in town became a bit more bearable.

Chapter 12

While you wouldn't think there was much time for anything other than eating, sleeping, working, and security, the heart finds a way to wiggle itself into the mix. There were folks pairing off, including the teenagers. However, with four teenage boys and only one teenage girl on the farm, the competition was fierce. Matt and Nick didn't seem particularly interested in Shannon; more like they were interested in giving Rusty and Ben a hard time about it.

When Shannon showed up with her family, there was a marked change in our teenage boys. They seemed more concerned about their appearance and when they weren't doing chores or working sentry duty, could usually be found in her vicinity. They began to argue over little things and seemed to be growing apart. I brought it up to Russ one evening while we were lying in bed not sleeping because it was sweltering in the room.

"I hope they won't let a girl destroy their friendship. They've been friends almost since they were babies. Maybe we should talk to Rusty."

"Stay out of it, Anne. They'll work it out or they won't. I'm pretty sure their friendship is strong enough to get through this, but you meddling in it won't help. In fact, it could make it worse."

"How so? I just want my son to be happy. How could I make it worse? What if he needs to talk to someone? I want him to know he can talk to us about this or anything."

Russ turned to look at me. "What do you know about being a teenage boy?"

I paused, then said, "Nothing, but—"

"Nope, stop right there. You cannot understand what he's going through. If he wants to talk to anyone, it will probably be me. And that will be on his time, not mine, or yours. Now, try to get some sleep."

I huffed. "In this heat? Doubtful."

He smiled, kissed me and rolled onto his side. "Night babe. I love you."

"I love you, too." I rolled onto my side as well. A thought hit me and I looked over my shoulder at him. "You'll tell me if he talks to you though, right?"

He laughed. "Yes, dear, I'll let you know. Good night."

****

"You're a dick, Rusty. Get away from me. Leave me alone!" Ben stormed off to the sound of Rusty's laughter and Shannon's giggling.

"That was mean, Rusty," Shannon said, trying to be serious. "Guys don't want other people to know stuff like that."

Rusty was still laughing as he watched Ben stomp up the porch stairs into the house. "Well, it's not my fault he peed the bed until he was ten. It's not like he still does it—I don't guess." He grinned at Shannon, who smiled back. "Anyway, he'll get over it. You wanna go see the baby goats?"

She nodded. "Oh yes, they're so cute!" They walked toward the barn together, talking about their lives before the pulse, and what they missed from then.

"I really miss gaming," Rusty said, "and talking to my friends online."

"Yes! And texting. And selfies!" She held up an imaginary phone over their heads. They both stuck their tongues out as she pushed the imaginary button to take the imaginary photo. She pretended to show him the phone, at which point they both laughed and continued walking. "Do you think that stuff will come back, Rusty? I mean, if we had it once, we should be able to have it again, shouldn't we?"

He was slowly shaking his head. "Honestly, I don't know. My dad thinks we will, but he said it could be years. Like, we could be grown-ups before we get the power back."

"Years? Oh my God! That's like forever!"

"I know," Rusty replied. "We could be as old as our parents even."

The shocked look on Shannon's face said that she hadn't considered the situation could last that long. "Wow. I guess I never thought about the power not coming back in like a few months. That sucks."

"Yep, sure does."

"But, why will it take years? I mean, when the power went out from a storm, it was back on in no more than four or five hours, and that's if the storm was really bad. Why is this going to take so long?"

Rusty looked at her. "Well, from what my dad told me, the EMP took out all the transformers and sub stations and everything. Those things are real expensive, so there aren't a bunch of replacements sitting around to fix the broken ones. Plus, the plants that make them don't have power if they're in this country, and we'd need to get them from some other country that still has power and could make them. Then, we'd have to wait for them to come over on cargo ships. Once they got here, we have another problem: the trucks that we need to haul them everywhere don't run. We're kind of screwed from all directions."

Shannon looked dejected. "Now I'm depressed. And that's something else I miss—chocolate! Chocolate always makes me feel better when I'm sad. Oh, what I wouldn't give for some dark chocolate."

Rusty grinned at her. "Let me talk to my mom. She has some of just about everything stashed somewhere. Maybe she has some."

"Oh, Rusty, that would be awesome! Yes, please ask her!"

He gave her a thumbs-up. "You got it."

****

From the kitchen, we heard the door slam then feet running up the stairs. Millie looked toward the front of the house. "What in the world? Sounds like an elephant going up the stairs."

I went to the living room and heard a door slam upstairs. I went up and the only door that was shut was the boys' room. I knocked softly. From inside, Ben yelled, "Go away!" I opened the door a little and looked in. He was lying on his bed facing the wall with a pillow over his head. I stepped in, closed the door, and walked to where he lay.

"Ben, what's wrong? What happened?"

He pulled the pillow tighter to his head. "I don't want to talk about it! Leave me alone! Please!"

"Ben, you know I'm not going to leave until you tell me what's wrong. Would you rather talk to your mom, or your dad?"

"I don't want to talk to anyone!"

I sighed. "Ben, we're in too tight of quarters here for there to be problems between people. Now tell me what you're mad about. I mean it!" I changed to mom-in-charge voice for that last part.

He snatched the pillow off his head and looked at me with eyes full of rage. "Your son and his big mouth! That's what I'm mad about!"

I was shocked. "What do you mean? What did he say?"

With angry tears coursing down his face, Ben lowered his voice and replied, "He told Shannon about me wetting the bed until I was ten. And he laughed about it to my face."

Now I was the angry one—at my son. "Oh honey, I'm so sorry. He had no right to do that. He'll be punished for it, I promise you that."

Ben shook his head. "It doesn't matter, Aunt Anne. It's done. She'll probably laugh about it every time she sees me now." He looked like his heart was broken and I'm sure it was.

"It does matter. I'll talk to Shannon, too. There were medical reasons for your problem and Rusty damn well knows that. I won't stand for him acting that way. You stay here until you calm down. He *will* apologize to you, in front of her."

I stormed out of the room, preparing to go to the door and yell for Rusty. As luck would have it, he was coming in with Shannon. The smile on his face immediately faded when he saw the mom look. I was livid, but I tried to calm myself. "Rusty, come with me. Shannon, please excuse us." I jerked my head toward the stairs. Looking down at his feet, Rusty slowly started climbing. I gave him a little shove and hissed through clenched teeth, "Get your ass to our room *now!*"

He walked into mine and Russ's bedroom, turned to face me, and immediately started making excuses. "Mom, it was an accident; it just kind of slipped out."

With my hands on my hips, I glared at him. "If it was an accident, why were you laughing?"

Now Rusty was getting perturbed. "I can't believe he ratted me out. Some friend …"

"Friend? *Friend?* What kind of friend are you? You embarrassed him in front of Shannon! How do you think you'd feel if the shoe was on the other foot?"

"But I didn't wet the bed."

"You sucked your thumb until you were six, right before you met Ben. Do you think it would be funny if that were told to Shannon? Not only that, but you know Ben had a bladder problem that took surgery to correct. He had no control over it. Now why would you do that to him, your *supposed* best friend?"

"I told you, Mom, it just slipped out. Besides, he called me a dick. That wasn't nice either."

I stopped for a moment. "No, it wasn't, but unfortunately it's true. I'm very disappointed in you, Rusty. You will apologize to Ben, in front of Shannon. You will explain that it was a medical condition. And you are on rabbit hutch and chicken coop cleaning duty for two weeks. Every day, by yourself."

His eyes got wide. "What? That's the little kids' chores."

"Well, maybe when you stop acting like a little kid, you'll be treated like the young adult you are supposed to be. I want you to stay up here and think about what you've done to a boy who has been like a brother to you almost your entire life because you were trying to impress a girl. When you come down, be ready to try to fix this. Do you understand me, young man?"

With his head down, he softly replied, "Yes ma'am. And Mom?"

"What?"

"I'm sorry I disappointed you."

I headed for the door. "I'm sorry you did, too."

****

As happens with kids, Ben forgave Rusty easily, which seemed to impress Shannon, so much so that she and Ben began spending quite a bit of time together alone. Trips to pick berries or gather apples became longer and longer. Rusty was crushed at first. His attempt to secure her affections by trying to make Ben look less of a man in her eyes apparently backfired and made her draw closer to Ben. But his brotherly love for Ben, his best friend for most of his life, won out over his puppy love for Shannon. Seeing them together, he knew what they shared was something special.

I was walking back from the chicken coop after checking on a batch of new chicks when Rusty came up to me. "Mom, can I ask you a question?"

"Of course, honey. What's up?"

"How do you know when you're really in love?"

I stopped in my tracks. "Wait, what?"

He laughed. "Sorry, didn't mean to freak you out."

Making sure my heart continued to beat, I replied, "No, no, it's okay, you just caught me off guard. Um, let's go sit at the table."

We walked over to the table and sat down across from each other. "So, what's brought this on?"

He looked down. "I thought I was in love with Shannon, I really did. My stomach did this fluttery thing whenever I saw her. But now, she looks at Ben the way I think I looked at her. And he looks at her the same way. I thought I was in love but I guess she wasn't. Not with me anyway."

A mother's instinct is to protect her children—from harm, from pain, anything and everything. I had a slight twinge of anger at this young woman who had broken my son's heart; maybe bruised it anyway. But you can't help who you fall in love with. It wasn't her fault. I looked at my son, almost a man, which was scary enough. Yet that little boy who used to pick weed flowers and bring them to me, who crawled up in my lap to snuggle when he was sick, who stuffed dozens of rocks in his pockets that didn't always get discovered before entering the washing machine—he was there as well. I struggled for the right words to ease his pain and prepare him for the right girl to come along.

"Well, I think sometimes it's hard to know if it's love, or lust, or attraction, or infatuation, at least at first. Your dad and I hung out as friends before we started dating. We went to movies, talked on the phone all the time, studied together, those kinds of things. When we finally figured out we wanted to start dating, be a real couple, we already knew each other so well, it was just a natural progression. Your dad is my best friend, and he feels the same about me. There is nothing we don't know about each other. For me, I knew when I looked at him one day and saw us as an old married couple, sitting on a porch, with grandkids running all over. I could see it as clear as I can see you right now. So, it may be different for everybody. I just know what it was for me."

Rusty looked thoughtful. "What about Dad? When did he know?"

I giggled. "According to him, it was with the first taste of my turkey and dressing. Which is probably why every year at Thanksgiving he proclaims, 'I'd marry you again for this dressing!'"

We both laughed at the memory of the annual occurrence. After a moment, he said, "Do you think I'll know, Mom? When the right one comes along?"

I reached across the table for his hand. "Without a doubt, honey. Your heart won't let you down."

He nodded his head, got up, walked over to me, and wrapped me in a hug. I hadn't gotten a hug like that from him in a long time. When he finally released me, he looked down at my face (when did he get so tall?) and with a smile replied, "Thanks Mom. Love you."

I replied with my standard, "Love you more." He walked away, leaving me there to contemplate the fact that my little boy was becoming a man. I don't think I was any more ready for that than I was to live without electricity. I had the same amount of control over both. None.

Chapter 13

Les walked out of the office he had taken for himself, his perpetual bad mood apparent on his face. The store they had boarded up to look vacant was still working as a living and storage facility. There was a distinct smell of unwashed bodies permeating the area, an issue that added to his discontent. *If we're all gonna keep living here, these jerkwads are gonna have to find a way to wash their nasty asses.* To make matters even more irritating for him, since their run from the confrontation with the people from that last neighborhood, his men had been less than enthusiastic about any more looting. Ray offered his reasoning for their stance.

"Les, man, we got tons of supplies. We don't have to take chances like that no more. We lost two guys out there. There ain't no reason to lose anybody else."

Les shoved him away, the smell of sweat and filth almost too much for him to bear. "Yeah, right, we got tons of supplies. The food might last us six months, maybe up to a year. Even gettin' rid of those skank bitches ain't gonna make that much difference. What happens then? You think the stores are going to magically fill back up? Or were you not planning to live longer than that? And what about water? Have you found some magical fountain that's flowing without electricity? Obviously not, from the way you look and smell. Get it through your thick skull, dumbass. There ain't no more deliveries. There won't be any manufacturing plants making canned corn or chicken noodle soup. Whatever is out there is all there is. If we don't get it now, someone else will. So, you'd rather fight people for their supplies than get them the easy way, from the places nobody came back to? Think! This is the easy pickings. It's only gonna get harder the longer this lasts."

Ray glanced down at his filthy shirt and jeans. "Well, when we find some water we don't need to drink, I might be able to wash up some. Hey, what about that place that was locked up tight as a fortress? We never went back there. I bet there's something really good in there, or in one of those houses beside it. It ain't but a couple of miles from here. You know those guys ain't there no more. Hell, there wasn't hardly anybody on that street anyway. We should go check that out."

Les considered what he had said. "Yeah, I guess we could go over there. Probably ain't nobody left but those morons that got in our business that one day. Maybe we can find a mud puddle for you to wash some of that filth off in. Muddy water is better than no water when you smell as bad as you do." He looked around at his gang and raised his voice so they could all hear him. "That goes for the rest of you, too! Everybody is gonna find a way to wash up today, or you're gonna be sleeping outside. It smells like a sewer in here. Get up! We're heading out!" He kicked the legs of the nearest guy sitting on the floor as he stormed off to his room.

Dave jerked his legs out of the way and rubbed the spot where he had just been kicked. He watched Les go to the office and slam the door. He looked up at Ray, apprehension apparent on his face. "Is this gonna be cool? Do you think there are any people there?"

Ray shook his head, still eying the door Les had slammed. "I don't know, man, but we were over there a lot in the beginning and no one screwed with us. Seems like it's safer to go somewhere we've been and didn't get shot at than somewhere we haven't been and God only knows who might be there. I ain't looking to get killed over some mac and cheese. And what's he talking about, saying this place smells like a sewer? I don't think it's that bad."

Dave shrugged. "Dunno. But, he keeps all those wet wipes we find for himself, ya know. How are we supposed to clean up when we gotta save all the water for drinking? They say when you smell yourself, everybody else has been smelling you for a long time. Maybe we're immune cuz we all stink. I wouldn't mind getting a rinse off, that's for sure. Wonder what we can use?"

Ray pulled his shirt front up to his nose and sniffed it. His face changed as he got up close and personal with his own stench. "Yeah, maybe we are a bit rank. We'll check toilet tanks, see if there's anything in 'em. That water was clean when everything went down. Be cleaner that what might be in the bowl, for sure. It won't do no good to wash up with shit water."

Dave snickered as he stood up. "We really would smell like a sewer then, huh?"

Ray grinned, then nodded somberly. "Yeah, and we'd be out on our asses. Keep your eyes open for anything we can use while we're out today. The less he has to bitch about, the better our lives are."

Dave reached down and rubbed the spot again where Les had kicked him. "You ain't lyin', brotha."

****

Alan, Steve, and Rich had skirted around town and hit the interstate. They figured they'd be better off out of the county, and Alan knew if he was going to find more like-minded guys, it would probably be closer to the city. Steve was still voicing his concerns regarding the plan.

"Al, how do you know any other gangs are gonna want to join up with us? There's only three of us, and Rich is still in pretty rough shape. I'm afraid they're going to look at how small our group is and just kill us outright. What do we have to offer them?"

Alan turned to him with a sinister grin. "The location of the gold mine, of course. No one else knows where that place is or

193

what they have in there. That's our bargaining chip. They'll be more than happy to bring us into the fold when we tell them about that place."

Steve looked confused. "But, *we* don't know what they have in there either, Al. What are we gonna tell them? That they *might* have a lot of food and guns and ammo? That there *might* be women and kids?"

"No, we're gonna tell them we know that they *do* have all those things. I ain't gotta see it to know they are protecting some mighty valuable items in there. What, do you think they'd go to all that trouble to hide the place if there was nothing in there worth taking?"

Steve slowly nodded. "I guess you're right. But you know we're gonna need a whole bunch of guys to get in there—like two dozen at least. You think we can find that many?"

"We just need to find one group of guys, maybe six or seven in their gang. Add those to ours and we're close to double digits. Then, we draft whoever we find running solo, if there's any still alive. You'd probably have a better chance solo, if you could dodge the bad guys. You know, the ones like us." He grinned at Steve, showing the damage the meth was already doing to his teeth. Steve gave him a half-hearted smile in return. Alan shook his head and continued. "By yourself, you'd only have one mouth to feed, so you wouldn't have to find as much food and shit, but you'd be sleeping with one eye open. There's bound to be some of those kind of guys out there, maybe tired of going it on their own, looking for a group to hook up with. I bet we could grow the group to like two dozen in no time. The biggest issue is going to be with the first group we hook up with though. Once we get past that, we should be good to go."

"What issue is that, Al?"

Alan swerved around a dead SUV. When he got back on the road, he looked at Steve and said, "Them dealing with the fact that I'm in charge."

****

Dead cars were everywhere but Alan was able to make his way through. They came to the strip mall just as another carload of guys were leaving the parking lot. The two groups stopped their vehicles in the middle of the road and stared at each other through their grimy windshields.

"Well, well, well, look what we have here. Potential recruits." Alan's smug tone put Steve on alert that trouble was probably on its way—or already there. Alan reached for the door handle with his left hand, while pulling his pistol with his right.

"What are you doing, Al? We don't know anything about those guys. Don't you think you should stay in the truck and wait to see what they do?"

Alan sneered at Steve. "You really are a whiny little bitch, you know that? If I confront them, I'm the alpha, you dumb shit. I'm taking charge. Just get your piece out and watch my back. C'mon."

Steve got out on the passenger side as slowly as he could without raising Alan's ire. He left the door open and tried to stay behind it as Alan sauntered toward the other truck. The driver got out with his pistol pointed at Alan, then quickly at Steve, then back to Alan.

"That's far enough, asshole! Who are you? What are you doing here? This is our territory! You wanna live, you'd best get back in that piece of shit truck of yours and get the hell out of here!"

Alan stopped but made no move to turn around. "Ya know, that's no way to talk to your future business partner. I take it you're the boss of this crew?" he said, inclining his head toward the man's truck.

"Yeah, I'm the boss and I ain't looking for no partner. I told you once to get out of here. I won't tell you again!"

By this time, men were climbing out of the cab and bed of the other truck. Steve counted six. Two to one—definitely outnumbered. Again.

Alan continued to stand there with an unmistakable smile. "Well, you have a nice sized crew there. Is that all of them?"

"No, this ain't all of them, and what business is it of yours? Are you an idiot or something? How many times do I have to tell you to get lost?"

At this point, the man's face was beet red and he was spitting the words out. He raised his gun and pointed it at Alan. Alan raised his hands, still smiling. "I think you might want to hear me out. I've got some information on a rich score."

The man seemed to consider what Alan had said, then let his gun drop slightly. "Well, if it's such a great score, why would you tell someone else about it? Why wouldn't you keep it to yourself?" he said, with a distinctly mistrustful tone. He narrowed his eyes and asked, "What's the catch?"

Alan leaned nonchalantly against the front fender of his truck, wiping the sweat from his brow. "See, I figured you for a smart guy and I was right. You got a place somewhere around here we can sit down and talk, maybe in the shade? It's kinda hot out here in the sun."

The man laughed. "What, you think we're just gonna take you back to our place, so you can see what we got and where we got it? Do I look stupid to you? Hell no. You want shade? Pull over under them trees there." He pointed past Alan to a small stand of trees on the corner.

Alan looked over his shoulder to where the man had indicated, then back. "That'll work. Let's get out of the middle of the road. Ya never know when someone might drive by, see our trucks parked here, and wonder what's going on."

The man turned toward his truck and replied, "Wonderin' that myself."

****

Alan introduced his men and Les did the same. Still wary, he looked at Alan. "So, where's this rich score anyway? Is it close?"

Alan smirked. "Slow down there, buddy. We're gonna have to go over a few things before we get to the good stuff. So, how many more guys you got? Cuz this ain't no little job."

Les hesitated for a second, then said, "I got four more guys back at our place, watching our stuff. How many more you got?"

Alan waved a hand at Rich and Steve. "This is it. That's why we're looking to take on some more guys. This is too much for just us three."

"How much is too much? What exactly is it we're looking at here?"

"Food, guns, women, kids—if that's your taste. Enough to last for years."

Les eyed Alan. "Where is this place? I'm bettin' it's pretty well guarded."

Steve watched and waited for Alan's response along with the other men. Alan never missed a beat.

"It's south of here, about thirty miles. Back in the country, lots of farmland. Yeah, they got some guards, but we already took out two of them. There's probably a dozen or so left."

"Probably? You don't know how many people they have? Have you seen this place or not?"

Alan continued his tale. "Yeah, I've seen it. It's just been a few days. I got no idea if everybody that was there before is still there. They had some neighbors staying with them, they could be gone home by now. We'll know for sure when we get there."

Les was shaking his head. "We ain't goin' nowhere until we know what we're walking into. We're gonna wanna go scope it out. We'll head out in the morning. We'll meet you guys here."

Alan showed the first sign of emotion—anger. "So, I offer you a piece of a rich deal, and you won't even put us up for the night? Tell ya what—we'll go find some other guys to partner with. Someone with manners, who'll appreciate this offer. Y'all can go fuck yourselves. C'mon guys, we're outta here."

Alan turned around and winked at Steve. He was headed toward his truck when Les called out. "Hold up! No reason to get pissy. You can crash with us tonight. I gotta warn ya though, the place is gettin' pretty rank. Ain't no water for bathin' or washin' clothes."

Alan spun back to Les. "There's a creek about two miles south of here. That should help with the cleaning up. I'm guessin' y'all got water for drinkin', cookin'?"

"Yeah, we save up all we find for drinkin'. That's why they smell so bad."

Alan laughed. "Y'all must be city boys. I bathed many a time in a creek in the summer. I wouldn't drink that water, mind ya. Ain't no tellin' who all's been washin' their ass in it. Course, if you ain't got none, ass water is better than no water." He continued to laugh at his own joke. A couple of Les's guys snickered, but a glare from Les silenced them.

"Okay, lead the way to this creek. We brought soap just in case we found a water source to use to clean up. Then we'll head back to our place and get some food, and you can tell us more about this *gold mine*."

They got into their respective vehicles to head out. Steve questioned Al, knowing it could be dangerous but curiosity got the better of him. "They're going to want details, Al. What are you gonna tell them?"

Alan smirked at him. "Whatever pops into my head. It don't matter, idiot. We just need them to get on board with the attack. Once we have the place under our control, we'll get rid of them anyway."

Yeah, no way this can go bad. Steve shook his head slightly and turned to watch the road go by.

****

That's exactly how the meeting went. Alan raved about the military grade weaponry, as well as tons of food to be had at the farm. He told them there were at least a dozen fine women there. He promised the availability of solar power so that hot showers could be had. That one peaked Les's interest as much as any of them.

"No shit! Running water? *Hot* running water? Man, a hot shower would rock! Alright, me and my guys are in. Here's what we should do—"

Alan interrupted him. "Yeah, I'm gonna go ahead and stop you right there. The only way this works is if I run the show. I lead, you and your guys follow." He didn't say anything else, waiting to see how Les would react. He wasn't surprised with what he got.

"*'Scuse me?* What the hell are you talking about? How exactly do you become the leader? You've got two guys. I've got ten. Pretty sure I've got the majority vote, ain't that right boys?"

He looked to his crew and was met with a chorus of "Hell yeah!", "You're the man, Les!" as he expected them to reply. He turned back to Alan with a smug look. Alan just smiled.

"Hey, that's cool. We'll find another crew that wants in. Thanks for dinner, fellas. Good luck. Let's go." He got up, gave a jerk of his head toward the door to Steve and Rich, and headed that way. His guys stood obediently and followed. They were almost to the door when Les yelled.

"Hold on a damn minute, would ya? We can talk about this."

Alan turned and looked at him. "No, we can't. This ain't negotiable. I'm the boss or we keep lookin' for some guys that want in. Your choice."

Les stood there, glaring at Alan. When it seemed he wouldn't capitulate, Alan turned back to the door.

"Fine! Fine! Alright, you're in charge. But this better be all you say it is." He left the challenge hanging in the air.

Alan ambled back to where Les was standing with his crew. Leaning over into his face, he replied calmly, "Are you threatening me, buddy?"

Les stood toe to toe with him. "Nah, that ain't a threat. We good. When are we gonna do this?"

Alan took a step back and laid his hand on Les's shoulder. Squeezing a bit too hard, he said, "Soon. We just need to work some shit out. If it's alright with you, me and my guys will crash here until we get ready to make our move. Cool?"

To his credit, Les didn't flinch. "Sure, Al. Cop a squat wherever you want." He ducked out of Alan's grasp and addressed his men. "Al here is going to lead the raid. He'll let us know when and where. I'd suggest everybody get some sleep. We're going to be busy real soon."

He turned and went to his office without another word.

Alan looked at Steve with a grin. "See? That wasn't so hard now, was it?"

Chapter 14

Water is life. Without water, we can't exist. Our bodies are more than half water. The earth is 70 percent water. Water makes plants grow, plants that provide the oxygen we breathe. Plants we can eat, and animals eat; then we eat the animals. Or animals that live in water that can become food. It almost always comes back to water.

The lack of fresh water had likely caused a lot of death in the months after the power went off. Thirst is a powerful motivator that can make people try any available source to quench it. Most people, especially the younger ones (including young adults), don't know anything about purifying water—or don't know they have to. They take for granted that the water will always come out of the faucet when you turn it on and that it's safe to drink. It's been that way their whole lives. They don't understand the processes said water has gone through to be a viable source that won't make them sick.

We had water available to us. We even had it inside the house. But no hot water, not without boiling it. No hot showers, no long soaks in the tub—at least, not without boiling a whole lot of it first, and then what about the other two dozen people there? But I really, really missed hot running water, so I was kind of a nag about it.

"Honestly, baby, I think we should prioritize the solar setup for power to the house. Running water would help so much. Hot running water would be the best! I don't know about you, but I feel like I have a permanent funk smell going on all the time."

Russ laughed at the face I made as I took a whiff of my shirt. "I feel your pain, but in the grand scheme of things, the refrigerator and freezer are a better use of electricity than the water heater. The ceiling fans seem to be a good choice as well. Maybe we can figure something else out for showers. Let's go talk to Mike and Monroe about it."

I put on my pouty face, which made Russ laugh again, but he continued on his way out the door. I grudgingly followed him. Apparently, I was not going to get my way on this one. Dammit.

We caught up to Mike and Monroe by the car shed. They were checking our reserves on gas and diesel and not looking very happy about it.

"Ya know, a thousand gallons sounds like a lot when you buy it but when you start using it on a regular basis, it goes pretty quick." Monroe appeared disgruntled as he said it.

Mike nodded. "Yeah, we've burned through a good bit of diesel driving over to Jim's place and working his fields. The sheriff said he'd reimburse us the fuel. We should probably take him up on that."

"You're damn right we should. Let's head over there and talk to him now."

Russ interjected, "Before we do that, we need to talk about a problem we have and see if we can come up with a remedy for it."

Mike looked at Russ. "What's the problem?"

I leaned around my husband and replied, "We smell. Bad."

Monroe raised his arm and sniffed his armpit. He looked at me and said, "I don't smell nothin'."

Russ and Mike laughed. Mike replied, "That's because you can become immune to your own body smells. Your brain adapts to it because it's always there. I'm sure only taking sponge baths we are all getting pretty ripe."

Russ continued. "I was thinking if we could come up with something along the lines of the camp showers we have, just a whole lot bigger, we might be able to actually shower from time to time." He turned to me. "Not every day, Anne. Not even every other day. But maybe once a week each would be better than not at all."

I was crestfallen. I hadn't had a decent shower since the morning the power went off. I'm pretty sure if I had known it was going to be the last real one I'd have for a while, I would have stayed in longer. The camp showers had been relegated to heating water for washing dishes, so we didn't have to use the gas stove to heat water—propane being another resource that would eventually disappear. We could have used the wood-burning stove, but with temps in the upper eighties to low nineties, with 70 percent humidity, no one wanted a fire anywhere near us. My expression most assuredly told the story of my disappointment.

Mike had that look on his face; the one that said, *I'm building something in my head.* I loved that look. It usually meant we'd end up with something cool and useful. Monroe must have seen it too. "What ya buildin' in that head of yours, Mike? We got the stuff here to do it?"

Mike slowly nodded and smiled at us. "I think I can come up with something. Let me work on it. In the meantime, let's go see Sheriff Burns about some go juice."

****

Gary was more than happy to supply us with fuel, both gasoline and diesel. Mike wasn't happy about having to "unlock" the front gate—that being removing the big log that was sunk in the ground behind the gate itself—but if that's what had to be done to replenish our reserves, so be it. Fuel tanks had been loaded onto pickup trucks and trailers and brought to the gates. However, no one was allowed inside except the sheriff. All other drivers were told to wait by the road while our people took their vehicles inside to add the fuel to our reserves. There was more than one person who seemed perturbed by this. Silas was among them and the most vocal about it.

"I'm not letting you take my truck in there without me. What's the big secret? I've been here before."

Monroe replied, "You ain't been here in years, Silas. Lots changed since then. We ain't as hospitable as we used to be."

Silas was trying to look around Monroe, peering to see past the gate area. Mike stepped in front of him. "I assure you, nothing will happen to your truck. We'll run it in, drain the tanks, and get it right back out here. Fifteen, twenty minutes, tops."

Silas opened his mouth to continue arguing but Gary interrupted him. "It's fine, Silas. They've already helped us out a ton with the work they've done on the gardens. Don't be an ass."

Mike turned his head with a snort but Monroe laughed out loud at the comment. "He can't help it, Gary. Once an ass, always an ass."

Face turning red, Silas spluttered out, "You can't talk to me like that! How dare you! Forget it! I'll just take my truck back to town and—"

Gary looked at him sternly. "Not with the town's gas on it you won't. Now, hand over your keys—unless you weren't planning to eat any of that food we're growing."

Silas stood there defiantly, seeming to be warring with himself over what to do next. Reluctantly, he handed his truck key to the sheriff. "Fine. But if anything happens to my truck …" He left the statement hanging.

"Good Lord, Silas, ain't nothin' gonna happen to your truck," Monroe said with a hint of exasperation. "Just have a seat over there in the shade. We'll be right back."

Silas huffed loudly and went to the spot Monroe had indicated. Gary handed the keys to Mike. "Take your time. No need to rush. It's not like he has any place else to be."

Monroe cackled. "Yeah, Mr. I-Own-My-Own-Business-So-I'm-Important ain't so much anymore, huh?"

Silas snapped his head around toward Monroe, but he had already climbed in the passenger side of the truck. They could hear Monroe laughing as the truck went down the driveway.

"Crazy old coot," Silas said under his breath, but loud enough for Gary to hear. Gary turned to him with a smile.

"The people here need nothing from us while we need so much from them. That doesn't sound crazy to me. That sounds pretty damn smart."

Silas mumbled under his breath but said nothing else aloud. Gary shook his head and turned back to Russ. "Please forgive his rudeness. The town is eternally grateful for all you folks have done."

"You're welcome, Gary. How's it going over there? Anything coming up yet? Yours is a good six weeks behind ours."

"Good, good. We're getting some nice leafy greens now. I think between what we've grown and what the hunters have brought in, we have some folks actually putting some weight on. I think if our canners can get enough put back, we may actually make it through the winter. I don't guess I have to ask how you all are doing in the food store department."

Russ smiled at him. "Yeah, I think we're covered for this winter, possibly the next couple. Oh, Anne said you guys were starting some firearms training in town. How's that going?"

Gary replied, "Good as well. We've got a few folks who don't have guns yet, but I've got extras at the office, and a couple of people in town have donated a few. We should be able to help a few of the folks out that need it the most."

Russ nodded, concern on his face. "Anne told me what prompted it. Honestly, I'm surprised there hasn't been more of it, especially for the single women."

"Unfortunately, a lot of women think it's their fault when a rape occurs, which couldn't be farther from the truth. They're ashamed and don't want anyone to know. There may have been more we just haven't heard about. I hope this training empowers everyone to stand up for themselves."

Ashley Dotson came over just then. "Excuse me, Sheriff. Is Tim around?"

Gary pointed to the end of the line of vehicles. "Yes'm, he's back there in my truck."

She smiled, said thank you, and headed that way. Gary's eyebrow shot up as he looked at Russ, who shrugged his shoulders then replied, "I can't keep up with it anymore, Gary. I just do what needs doing. But you know what they say, 'Love knows no bounds.' Or something like that. No idea when that happened though."

Gary grinned at him. "Yeah, I'm one to talk. I looked at the world around us, figured we might as well live for the day and married Angie. It could be that something like this makes you see what's really important in life and what isn't."

"Yep. Taking care of my family is the most important thing I have to do now. Keeping them sheltered, fed, and protected is my job. When life takes you back to the basics, and you realize fancy houses and fast cars mean nothing in a world like this one. Your perspective changes—for the good, I think."

Gary turned back to see Ashley standing beside his truck talking to Tim. They were both smiling and laughing. "That's the first time I've seen Tim laugh since this whole thing started. I think you might be right about those changes for the good, Russ."

****

Mike, Lee, and Bob worked diligently on a project over the next few days. Whenever I tried to see what they were doing they ran me off, saying I was going to spoil the surprise. I grumbled that I didn't like surprises, which wasn't true. I loved them. But I was also nosy. Finally, after much hammering, sawing, and welding, Mike called the group together.

"So, Anne has been begging to take a hot shower. I know she meant in the house in the tub, but I think we've come up with an alternative that will use no power outside of what the heat of the sun already provides. If you'll follow me."

He led us around to the other side of the outhouse where we found a new structure. It had two stalls with separate entries—so to speak. The stalls were wood on three sides with a shower curtain creating the fourth. Each stall had a pallet floor and a showerhead with a valve handle behind it. There were even hooks outside the shower curtain to hang towels and clothes on. Above and behind the stalls were four fifty-five-gallon drums painted black and standing on end on a tall platform. Two drums were plumbed together to give over a hundred gallons of water per stall. The showerhead was attached to a pipe, which was connected to the plumbing for the drums. Black plastic sheeting covered the drums as well. The platform built to hold the ton of water and containers consisted of six-by-six posts, reinforced with angle iron. Cross bracing helped to provide the stability needed for that amount of weight six feet off the ground. The platform landing was comprised of two-by-six boards with two-by-six supports every sixteen inches.

Monroe eyed it critically. "That's a hoss right there, fellas. How's it work?"

Mike started pointing to the different sections. "Rainwater enters the drums at the top. We've cut holes about six inches square in each one. The water will heat from the sun, aided by the black paint. I don't know if we'll ever get a *hot* shower, but it will definitely be warm. Once inside the stall, you turn the ball valve. That will open up the valve to let the water come out of the showerhead. I would suggest getting wet, closing the valve, soaping up, then rinsing off. This still isn't a whole lot of water for this many people. I think it will work though."

I was checking the setup closely. "What about bugs? Won't that water be a mosquito magnet?"

Bob replied, "We put screen in the holes to keep the pesky buggers out."

"What about in the fall when the leaves start dropping? Won't they clog up the holes?"

Lee answered that question. "If all goes well, we hope to have a roof over the drums before then. We have some roofing set aside. We'll add a gutter system to fill the barrels from the runoff."

"Well, looks like you boys thought it all through," Monroe said. "Anybody tried it yet?"

Mike laughed. "The barrels have only been set up for a couple of days and we haven't had more than a sprinkle. We'll have to wait for a good rain to get them filled. Then we'll need a couple of warm days to heat the water."

"Well, I reckon we'll find out soon enough. Looks like a thunderhead coming from the west. Lord knows the plants need the rain." Monroe was pointing to the western sky where it looked as if a summer storm was brewing.

I clapped my hands. "Oh, thank goodness. We haven't had rain in over a week. We were getting dangerously close to having to start hauling water to the gardens." I had no sooner gotten the words out of my mouth than there was a lightning flash, followed by a long rumble of thunder. Everyone's face lit up at the prospect of a good summer soaker coming. I was thinking about a soaker, too—in about two or three days under one of those shower heads. I went around and hugged each man. "Thank you so much for figuring this out for us, guys. I can hardly wait to try it out!"

We did indeed get the soaker. It rained hard at first, driving us all indoors, with thunder and lightning that was pretty intense. After that, we had a good steady rain for about two hours. The guys donned rain gear and went out to check the barrels. They were full. Two days later, I stepped in as the first person to use the shower set up. The water wasn't hot, as Mike had predicted, but after two days of high nineties following the rain, it was definitely warm. And it was glorious. I had to make myself not be stingy and use too much water because I could have stood there until it was gone. I had definitely missed hot … er, warm showers. The line formed when I got out. We deemed the drum showers a success.

Chapter 15

"The plan is simple. We go in shootin', they run, we take their stuff," Alan said with meth-induced pride.

"What the hell kind of plan is that?" Les asked, irritation evident in his tone, even though he had been high for the better part of the day. "You have no idea how many of them are in there. You can't see inside the place, so you don't know where they are either. And why would they run? It's their place. They know it better than anybody. Are you *tryin'* to get us killed?"

Alan laughed. "You sound like Steve. Y'all should get married; you're perfect for each other. We ain't goin' in broad daylight, idiot. We wait 'til just at dark. We go in through the back where we killed those guys. They piled shit up to make it look like there ain't a hole there, but there is. Then we split up, come at 'em from all sides. They won't be expectin' that. I'm bettin' they watch the front the most. Figure it's in people's nature to come in the front door. We're going in the front, the back, and both sides."

Les was shaking his head. "We've got what, ten, twelve guys, and that's if we pick up a few more on the way? They could have two or three times that many. Plus, they'd have the advantage because they know the place and we don't. Without knowing how many people are in there or what the layout is we could be walking into a massacre—ours. That's just crazy, man."

Alan eyed Les angrily. "Don't call me crazy."

"I didn't call you crazy. I said the plan is crazy."

"You got a better idea then?"

Les thought for a moment. *Is there a better plan? Is there a way to increase the chance of success and not get killed?* An idea came to him. "What about neighbors? Is there anybody around that maybe aren't friends with these people, that might have a beef with them? Maybe we can recruit some help close by that has some intel."

Now it was Alan's turn to look thoughtful. "Ya know, that's a damn good idea. We just happen to know someone personal who might can help. His name is Tim Miller. He's a sheriff's deputy. He's—"

"Okay, *now* I'm calling you crazy! You want to bring a sheriff's deputy in on this plan? Yeah, no way *that* can go wrong," he replied sarcastically.

Alan got up, strode across the room, and grabbed Les by the shirt front. He lifted him out of the chair and pulled him to his face. "I've had about all of the smart-ass comments I'm gonna take from you," he calmly stated. The threat was veiled but there. Les didn't comment, but seethed inside. *First chance I get, I'm takin' this asshole out.* Rather than voice his own threat, he gave Alan a curt nod. Alan let him go.

"Fine. We'll do it your way. Who cares if we all die. I didn't want to live forever anyway." Les straightened his shirt and turned to his men. "Looks like we're heading to town, boys. Load up on food, water, guns, and ammo. Oh, and booze. Lots of booze. I think we're gonna need it."

****

Alan pulled up about a mile outside of town. He got out of his truck and walked back to Les. "We're gonna need one or two of you to go to the sheriff's office and talk to Tim, get him to come out here. We can't really go into town. We left a trail of bad blood, if you know what I mean."

Les looked at Alan, exasperated. "And just how are we supposed to get him to come out here? He doesn't know any of us. He's liable to shoot us."

"He won't shoot you. He's basically a puss. Just tell him Al wants to talk to him. He'll come."

"So, what, we just walk up to the sheriff's office and ask for Tim? What if he ain't there and the sheriff is and wants to know who we are and why we want to talk to him?"

"Well, I guess you'll have to come up with something then, won't you. Do I have to plan the whole thing out for you? How did you make it this long without being able to actually *do* anything without someone telling you how to do it?"

Les was seething but didn't push Alan. Gritting his teeth, he said, "Yeah, you're right. We got this. C'mon, Ray, let's go."

Les and Ray set out toward town on foot. Alan followed until he reached his truck. He called after them, "Hurry up whenever ya can. I'm ready to get this party started!"

Les grumbled as they walked. It was hot and muggy, and he wasn't happy at all about walking down a road with no trees to provide any shade, sipping warm water, but most of all dealing with Alan. "That guy is the biggest pain in the ass I have ever met. Why did I agree to this whole merger thing? I swear, he's some kind of crazy psycho meth head. And I still think he's gonna get us all killed."

Ray was dragging his feet and stumbled over a rock. He flailed his arms trying to keep from falling. Les laughed at him. When he got his balance back, he replied, "Nice Les. Preesh. Anyway, if you feel that way, why are we doing this? Why don't we just go back to the plan to keep looking for empty houses? We were doing pretty good with that, and we still haven't got to go back to the one that was locked up so tight. Why don't we just pack up and leave?"

Les stopped and looked at Ray. "Because he's a crazy psycho meth head. He knows where we live. He knows how much stuff we've got. If he's willing to try to take this place out here, wherever it is, without knowing what he's up against, what wouldn't he do to take our stuff? Nah, we're in it now. Might as well finish it."

Ray was looking down to make sure he didn't trip again. "Yeah, if it doesn't finish us first."

Les nodded and kept walking.

When they got to town, they were surprised at how clean everything was. Unlike the area around the mall, the streets weren't full of litter and no one seemed to be using them as their personal toilet. They noticed that most of the houses on the street had neat little gardens where front lawns would normally have been. The people were not very friendly though. They were watching the two men carefully as they walked down the street. In the time before the pulse, these townspeople would have smiled and waved, calling out greetings to the strangers. Now, strangers were suspect and many of the residents were holding shotguns and rifles in plain view, as if to say, *Don't start no shit, won't be no shit.* Les gave curt nods to the ones who made eye contact with him as they continued toward the center of town.

Ray whispered, "Not a real friendly place, huh?"

"Nope, but can't say I blame them. The world has kind of gone to hell. Now there's guys like us running around everywhere." He grinned as he said it and Ray laughed.

"I guess you're right. Hey, at least we got to clean up before we came in, and don't look like homeless serial killers or something."

"Yeah, and don't smell like ass anymore. Well, not as bad anyway."

Ray lifted the front of his shirt to his nose and sniffed. "Definitely less gamey."

They followed the directions Alan had provided taking them right to the door of the sheriff's office. Once there, they hesitated about going inside. "Man, are we sure that asshole isn't setting us up to get busted so he can go back and steal our stuff?" Ray was worried, and it showed in his voice.

Les answered him. "I don't see how he could. He didn't know us or what we have until yesterday. He never left once we met them so there's no way he could have told anybody about us."

"Yeah, I guess you're right. It's still creeping me out though, walking into the cop shop on purpose."

Les reached for the door and found it unlocked. "Hmm. Al said the door was locked the last time he was here. Course, according to him, that's been a while. Let's go find this Tim dude."

They walked in to the dark interior of the office. They were met by a man holding a tactical shotgun. While it wasn't pointed at them, it was in a position that could quickly be brought up for business if needed. The man addressed them immediately.

"Help you boys with something?"

Les put a smile on his face. "Yes sir, we're looking for some-one. Name's Tim. Tim Miller. Is he around?"

The man eyed them warily. "I don't remember seeing you fellas around here before. What business do you have with Deputy Miller?"

"A friend of his said we should look him up. So, is he here?"

"What friend?"

Les was getting annoyed at all the questions. "Um, no offense, buddy, but we really need to be talking to Tim about this, not you. If he's not here, we'll go and come back later."

"You are talking to Tim Miller. What friend?"

Les stopped and took a good look at the man named Tim. He was short of stature and not muscular at all. However, he was clean and didn't look like he'd been missing any meals. Les stuck his hand out. "Well hey there, Tim. Name's Les. This here is my buddy, Ray. Alan sent us here looking for you. Said to tell you he wanted to talk to you."

Tim's eyes got big. He ignored the proffered hand. "Come outside." They followed him out the door and to the side of the building. "Al sent you? Where is he? He'd better not come to town. The sheriff is looking for him. He's in big trouble."

"Yeah, he figured as much. That's why he sent us. He's just outside of town. Said we should bring you back with us."

Tim was shaking his head. "No. No way! I'm not getting anywhere near Al or the rest of them. I'm done with those guys. I've got a sweet gig right here. As long as I protect and serve, I get a roof and food. That's more than a lot of folks have out there. I thought about doing some shady shit early on to get as much as I could, but I'm okay with the way things are now. You just go tell Al whatever he wanted from me he ain't gettin'."

Les replied, "He's gonna be pissed, ya know. What do you want me to tell him?"

Tim shrugged. "I don't really care. Things are different for me now. I'm the senior deputy. I've got a gal I'm seein'. I can't get involved in any of Al's bullshit. Tell him that I wasn't here. My girlfriend lives on a farm outside of town with a bunch of other folks, I could have been there. If you had shown up about ten minutes later I wouldn't have been here, I would have been out there with her. Or you can tell him I said no. It doesn't matter to me. Now you guys better get out of here. The sheriff don't take kindly to strangers in town."

Les didn't want to go back to Alan with nothing, so he decided to try to get the information they were after. "Wait, you say your girlfriend lives on a farm outside of town with others? How many others?"

Tim hesitated. "I don't know, like two dozen. Why? What's it to you?"

"And is the farm kind of hid from the road?"

Now Tim was looking suspicious. "How do you know that? What the hell are you and Al up to?"

Les smiled. "Oh nothing, just a story Al told us about having a run in with some folks on a farm. We're gonna go now. I'll tell Al you couldn't make it cuz you had deputy business to tend to but that you said to tell him hey. Nice to meet ya, Tim. Let's go, Ray."

Les and Ray hurried off with Tim staring after them. Les was almost giddy. Ray was confused. "Why the hell are you so happy, Les? He didn't come with us. Al's gonna be pissed."

Les leered at him. "You're such an idiot. That dumb ass deputy just told us what Al wanted to know. We don't need him now. We got the information."

"Yeah, we got that there's two dozen people out there. That means we're outnumbered at least two to one. Why is that good news?"

Les stopped for a moment, looked at Ray, then continued on toward their waiting crew. "We'll worry about that later. Two dozen people! Imagine how much food they have there. And hot water! We need this place. Al was right. This one is a gold mine!"

Ray mumbled to himself. "Lotsa folks die in mines. Just sayin'."

****

Alan watched as the two men walked back without Tim. *That pussy didn't come.* He was seething by the time they got to where the vehicles were parked. "Where the hell is he? Did you tell him I wanted to talk to him?"

Les held his hands up, trying to calm Alan down. "Hold on, Al. We saw him. He had sheriff business he was having to tend to. But it's okay, cuz he gave us the info we needed."

Alan looked at him with disbelief. "Now, how the hell would he know what we wanted from him? Did you ask him about the place?"

Les was almost giddy. "No, man, he told us by accident. He's messin' with a gal who lives out there! He told us they got about two dozen people."

Alan's eyes lit up. "Did he say how many was grown-ups, and how many kids? Did he say what the layout of the place is?"

Les shook his head. "No, I told you it was an accident. We didn't get no details. But we know how many, at least."

"And you know some of them are women and kids, so that makes the numbers even better. Yeah, this is looking good, real good." Alan's mood was improving as the scenario played out in his head. "We need to get a little closer to town, see if we can pick up a couple more guys. Then I think we'll be ready."

Steve looked at him suspiciously. "Ready for what?"

Alan grinned back. "Ready to take that damn farm."

****

Silas had complained to anyone who would listen about the ill treatment he received at the Warren place. Hanging out at Manchin's during a rain storm, he spent the afternoon bending Doug's ear. Most of the people he had complained to all but ignored him. Doug was a different story though. He had been shut out by everyone in town over the food hoarding after Gary released him and Kevin from jail. He was very interested in what was out there. He wanted to build up a new cache.

"They act like they've got some top-secret military facility out there or something," Silas said. "It's a farm, for God's sake! They've got pigs and cows and chickens. What's the big secret?"

"So, they wouldn't even let you through the gate?"

"No, but they sure took my truck in to get the fuel off of it. I'm telling you they've got something big out there."

"Big how?"

"I don't know. But it sure would be interesting to find out," Silas replied. Doug nodded in agreement.

Just then, a couple of strangers walked into the store. The men were not dirty, but not clean. Their clothes were tattered and they looked like they hadn't shaved since the power went off. They looked around, eyes wide. "Wow. Y'all got a nice setup here." The men leered at Staci at the counter. "Real nice."

Jesse stepped in front of his wife. "How can we help you?"

"Oh, we was just passin' through, maybe lookin' for a new place to settle down. This seems like a right fine little town y'all got here." He looked at the whiteboard on the wall behind the counter. "Wow, you got a nice offering of fresh meat. Y'all must be some good hunters."

Jesse eyed the men suspiciously. "Yes, we have some very good shooters living here. Did you want to trade for some meat or canned goods there?" He motioned to the wall behind Silas and Doug. "If not, you should probably move along. The sheriff isn't too fond of strangers being in town."

The man smiled at him. "Well, my name's Les and this here is my buddy Ray. Now, you tell us your names and we won't be strangers no more."

Jesse ignored the request. "Do you want to trade or not? If so, tell me what you want and what you have to trade for it. If not, you fellas need to move along."

Les seemed a bit perturbed. "Ya know, you ain't neighborly at all. Is this how you treat all your customers?"

"Unless you're trading, you ain't a customer."

"With an attitude like that, I don't believe I want to do business with y'all. We need to find our friends on the Warren farm anyway. C'mon, Ray, let's go."

At the mention of the Warren farm, Silas and Doug both sat up straight. Silas addressed the men. "You know Monroe Warren?"

Gotcha, thought Ray. Al was right. All he had to do was mention the name and he'd get someone's attention. Trying not to let his excitement show, he turned to the man who had spoken. "We're acquainted, yes. And you are?"

Ever the salesman, Silas stuck his hand out in greeting. "Silas. Silas Jones. Ray, right?"

Les shook his hand. "Les. That there is Ray. So, I guess you know the Warrens, too?"

"Of course. I know everyone in and around town. Their place is about five miles northeast of here. Nice farm."

"Have you been out there recently? It's been a few years for me."

"Why yes, I was out there just a couple of days ago. It's quite grown up now. If you didn't know where it was, you'd miss it. But I guess that was the point."

Les prodded the chatty man for more info. "What do you mean?"

"Well, they're very secretive about the place now; like they won't let anybody in, including me." In his self-important indignation, Silas rambled on. "I'm not really sure what the big deal is, but there was plenty of activity out there, from the little bit I could see from the gate."

"Oh yeah? Like what, milking cows, slopping the hogs?" Les elbowed Ray and they both laughed.

"I'm sure that was going on back at the barn. No, I'm talking about—"

"Silas, I'm sure these fellas need to be on their way." Jesse interrupted Silas before he could give the men any more information. "You boys don't want to be here when the sheriff comes around, which he does pretty much every day around this time."

Les gave Jesse a dirty look, then smiled at Silas. "Silas and—I'm sorry, I didn't catch your name?" He directed the question to Doug.

"I didn't throw it, but the name is Doug."

Les chuckled. "Right. Silas and Doug, would you two like to take a walk around with us? Show us the sights, so to speak?"

Silas beamed. "Of course, it would be our pleasure. C'mon Doug. See ya later, Jesse, Staci."

Jesse grimaced as Silas told the men their names. Les grinned at them, but there was no humor in the look. "Jesse. May we meet again." He then turned his gaze to Staci. "I certainly hope we meet *you* again, pretty lady."

Jesse pulled the shotgun he'd held at his side up so that Les could see it. "You won't. Get out. Now."

Les laughed as he opened the door and the four men walked out together. Staci looked at Jesse, disgust apparent on her face and in her tone. "That was gross. They were gross. Are you going to tell Sheriff Burns about those guys?"

Jesse stared daggers after the men as they walked down the street. "You bet your ass I am. Those guys are nothing but trouble, including Silas and Doug. What an idiot Silas is, telling all that about the Warren place. You don't tell stuff like that to strangers. And then he leaves with them? God only knows what else he'll tell them."

Staci shook her head. "My guess is everything he knows and then some. This is bad, right?"

"Yep. I'm going to find the sheriff."

****

Silas did indeed tell Les everything he wanted to know about the Warren farm, at least what he knew. He told them he had seen at least six men, although it could have been eight, as well as two women at the farm and another two at the Dotson place. He didn't know anything about them having running water but he related that the people and their clothing seemed clean so it was highly possible that was true. He didn't seem to realize Les was pumping him for information. Doug did.

"How come you're so interested in what they've got out there, how many people, that kind of stuff? I thought you knew them."

Les replied smoothly, "Not so much know as have heard about them and their set up. Seems like the place to be in a world like this."

Silas laughed. "They wouldn't let me in and I've known Monroe for years. If you don't actually know them, there's no way you're getting in."

Les just smiled. "We'll see. It isn't right for them to have so much when so many people are doing without."

Doug nodded his head. "I've said the same thing. People should be sharing with each other so everyone has the same. That's how neighbors are supposed to act."

Les nodded. "Yes, it is, and that's why we have a group of people who are willing to go out there and persuade these people to share in their bounty. Would either of you fellas be interested in joining us in this expedition?"

Silas looked skeptical, but Doug was all head bobs and grins. "Oh yeah, I would definitely be interested. Silas here has a truck that runs, too. We can help you fellas haul stuff out, if there's stuff to haul, which I'm bettin' there is. A lot."

Silas glared at Doug, as if to say, *What the hell, dude?* but said nothing. "Awesome. Let's get some plans made to visit these folks," Les said.

Doug followed Les eagerly. Silas was lagging behind. Ray nudged him. "Something wrong, Silas?"

Silas shook his head. "No, no, nothing wrong. Just wondering what type of persuasion was going to be used here."

Les turned around, walking backwards as he spoke. "We'll start with asking. See how that goes. From there, it gets messier."

Silas stopped in his tracks. "Messier?"

Les stopped as well, with a menacing look. "Yeah. You know, not nice. That's how this works. We ask, then we take."

Silas stood resolute. "I'm sorry, I can't do that. People will get hurt."

"Yes, they will. That's what happens in wars," Les said with a sneer.

"War? When did this become a war?" Silas asked incredulously.

Les turned back around and continued down the street. "When the lights went out."

****

Jesse started for the door just as Gary was walking in. "Sheriff, I was just coming to find you. I think there's some guys in town looking for trouble."

"Who were they? What makes you think they're trouble?" Gary asked.

"Their names were Les and Ray. Les was the one who did all the talking. They were looking around like they were casing the joint, including my wife. Said they were looking for a new place to settle down in. I told them they either had to trade with us or move on. Then they said something about going to find the Warren place and Silas was running off at the mouth telling them what he knew about the place. They just look like bad news to me."

Gary sighed. "When the good Lord was handing out smarts, I believe Silas thought he said farts and declined. That man just doesn't know when to shut up."

Staci giggled at Gary's comment, then said, "They were really creepy, Sheriff Burns. They made my skin crawl. I'm with Jesse— they are definitely up to no good."

"How long ago were they here? Which way did they go?"

Jesse pointed at the door. "They left about ten minutes ago, with Silas and Doug, heading away from town. There's no telling what all those two told them. Right before those guys came in, Silas was bitching and moaning about Monroe not letting him in the place. Doug was all up in that, agreeing that they treated him bad."

Gary had a grim look on his face. "I'm going to go see if I can catch them. Thank you for letting me know, Jesse, Staci. Stay safe. Keep that shotgun handy."

Jesse nodded as he raised the gun slightly. "Always."

Gary walked out the door and headed in the direction Jesse had indicated. He checked the side streets as he went but found no signs of Silas, Doug, or two men he didn't recognize. He didn't see them anywhere. After a couple of blocks, he said aloud, "Well, I guess I missed them. Better let Monroe and his crew know they may have some new trouble coming. And I'm talking to myself." He laughed, then turned back to get his truck.

****

"Alright, where's this truck of yours, Silas?" Les questioned as they turned the corner. "We can use it to go hook up with the rest of crew outside of town. Save us the walk."

"It's, um, just up the street there at my dealership. I have a nice couch in my office. Sometimes I sleep there just to keep an eye on things, then walk to Manchin's to save on gas. But, if it's all the same to you fellas, I believe I'll bow out of this excursion. I appreciate you wanting to include me, but I don't think this is something I can do."

Les stopped, put his hands to the small of his back and arched his back, creating a series of pops and cracks as the vertebrae realigned, then pulled a pistol from the waistband of his pants. Pointing it at Silas, he calmly replied, "Sorry, Silas, but you can't opt out of this gig. You know too much so either you're in or you're out—for good. Like dead. You feel me?"

Silas stared wide-eyed at the gun pointed at him. "Uh, yes … yes, I understand. But I don't know how much help I can be. I don't even own a gun. I've never had a use for one."

"Well see? Now you do. It's a dangerous world out there now, Silas. Everybody better have a gun—unless you want to end up dead or worse."

"What's worse than dead?" Silas asked, fear apparent in his voice.

Les laughed. "Ending up as somebody's bitch for one. Plus, how you gonna eat if you can't shoot deer and rabbits and shit? What, you gonna eat grass?"

Silas eyed the pistol that was still pointed at him. "Do you hunt with that gun?"

"Of course not, you idiot. You use a shotgun or a rifle."

"So, you fellas have been hunting for your food?" Silas questioned.

Now Ray laughed. "Yeah, you could say that. Huntin' in abandoned houses, anyway."

Les joined him in the joke. "And we only had to shoot a couple of stingy old people that had a sweet stash of food. So, don't think for a second I won't shoot you, Si. You're going with us. Let's get your truck and go hook up with the rest of our crew." He turned to Doug. "How 'bout you, bubba? You ready to do this?"

Doug nodded. "Yeah. Yeah, man, I'm in. I got no love loss for anybody in this place or close to it. Let's go."

Les grinned. "Now that's what I'm talking about. Let's roll, fellas!"

****

Alan had alerted the group that an unknown vehicle was approaching. They got behind their trucks and had their weapons drawn. The truck stopped about five hundred feet away. Everyone tensed up. Then Les climbed out of the cab and they relaxed. He waved, got back in and the truck continued toward them. When it reached their location, it stopped and Les and Ray got out with two strangers.

"Who you got with ya, Les? Recruits?" Alan asked.

Les nodded with a grin. "Yep, two new recruits that just happen to know the Warrens."

Alan's eyebrows shot up. "No shit? Well this is our lucky day then. What all did you tell them?"

Les reiterated the story, as well as Silas's reluctance to join the attack. Alan walked over to Silas, put an arm across his shoulders and squeezed tightly. "Just so we're clear. You're with *us* now. We'll be heading out to that farm at dusk. You'll be providing intel on what's inside. Let's get going. We're gonna set up a couple of miles from there until then."

Silas whimpered. "As I told your friend, I haven't been out there in years. The last time I was there, just a couple of days ago, they wouldn't let me inside. There were new people there I didn't recognize. I don't think I can be of any help to you. I can't shoot people. I can't even shoot. Please let me go. I won't tell anyone anything. I don't want any trouble."

Alan laughed. "Well, that's too bad, Si. Cuz you've got yourself a shit ton of it. Let's go."

Chapter 16

War had come to our soil. The UN peacekeepers had, with the current administration's blessing and backing of DHS, taken control of almost every major city in the country. Los Angeles and San Francisco on the west coast; Chicago in the Midwest; New York City, Boston, and Philadelphia in the northeast; Atlanta and Miami in the southeast; and of course, Washington D.C. They found out, though, that folks outside those cities weren't so easy to subdue. No, the regular people like us didn't have tanks or full auto guns—no matter what the liberal media had tried to make people believe in the past— but we had a fierce love of our freedom that we weren't ready to give up.

They tried the six-man teams going to door to door to confis-cate vehicles, food, guns, and ammo, just as we'd heard over the ham that night. They started just outside the bigger cities, with lists of names and addresses. Apparently, a lot of other folks were listening when we were and prepared for it. Older trucks and cars were partially dismantled and dusted to look unused. People were either hiding their supplies in buried caches or meeting the collectors with at least six armed men and women at the door. The message was unmistakable: we won't give up our guns without a fight. You won't control us by taking our food and supplies. You won't make us dependent on you or anyone else for our survival.

The president brought our troops home with the idea that they would assist the UN in gaining control over the populace. Quite the opposite, the men and women of our armed forces rebelled en masse when the order came down, up to and including the top brass. They scattered to the homes of comrades that were close, forming up into units. They brought as much gear as they could carry and set up camps. They kept their comms but used them to hear what the administration was up to, not to communicate with each other. The word spread that our troops had defected, and with bases all over the country, we quickly had a nice militia in place.

With Fort Campbell just a couple of hours north of us, the area was getting good saturation. Some of the soldiers from up there had made it into town looking for family members, who unfortunately hadn't come home. After talking to Gary, they set up in some of the abandoned family homes and offered their services as security for the town and the surrounding area. Gary told us he accepted immediately.

"These guys show up at my door wearing digital camo fatigues. I opened the door, and one of them said, 'Good morning, sir. Would you happen to be looking for a few good men? If so, I'm sorry, we're not the Marines. Would you be interested in a few so-so soldiers?' They all grinned then and I couldn't help but laugh." Gary shared the story with us at the gardens when we inquired about the new muscle he'd brought. "They check in with me every morning, bright and early. They help with firearms training, patrol the town, whatever we need them to do. We can barely get them to take food. They brought cases of MREs with them. Dane, their de facto squad leader, said they don't want to get soft with home-cooked meals until the fight is over."

"What fight?" Bob questioned, beating me to it.

"That's what I asked. He said, 'The one that's coming.' I said, 'Who with?' He said, 'The president, his administration, DHS, the UN—some or all of the above.' So, I guess what you all heard was true."

Mike had been talking to the soldiers, who we now knew as Dane, Conner, Evan, John, and Scott. He came over to us, a grim look on his face. "Yep, they were recalled from Afghanistan. They weren't told anything until they got back to the base. When everyone was home—I mean every troop we have—there was an announcement made by the president himself. He said their services were needed here at home to quell the lawlessness and gain control over the people and the resources they possessed so that we could win the fight against our real enemy."

I looked at him with confusion. "And who would that be?"

"Apparently whoever set off the EMP—except they aren't pointing any fingers at anybody. They haven't said who this alleged enemy is."

Now Russ got involved. "What are you saying, Mike? Or should I say not saying?"

Mike looked at all of us for a long time. Finally, he replied, "After talking with the fellas, and hearing what the administration didn't say, I have a guess."

He paused and we waited. Finally, Bob couldn't stand it any longer. "Well? What is it?"

He took a deep breath. "I think our government set off the EMP, or some faction of it."

"*What?* You're saying the president ordered this? But *why?*" Gary was as shocked as the rest of us.

Mike nodded grimly. "To do exactly what they were trying to order our troops to do. Control the people. Take away the guns, make them dependent on the government for basic necessities like food and water, and you have all the control you need. Use the UN to bring everyone in line, then DHS takes over with a contingent of UN soldiers left here permanently to back them up. No more local cops, or sheriffs," he said motioning to Gary, "or any local or state governments. And they almost did it without firing a shot."

"How so? I heard the people were fighting back. We sure in the hell would." The anger in Bob's voice was very apparent.

241

"Yeah, that's the almost part. The big cities were easy to take. Take out the gangs and the people who were left were so grateful that the government had finally arrived to protect and help them that they opened the door and invited them in. All of our major cities have become police states. Most of the residents have been ushered into FEMA camps. Once they started going outside those places looking for resources, and word spread about how they were doing it, the resistance formed. When the troops found out what they were brought home to do, all hell broke loose. Five-star generals walked out of the announcement meeting, along with all the admirals present. Apparently, the president mistook their oath to protect and defend as a promise to obey his every mandate. Militias are forming up all over the country, staffed with recently active military troops who brought goodies from the bases before the UN troops and DHS could lock them down. When news gets out that our own government is responsible for putting us in this position, we're going to have a cross between the Revolutionary War and the Civil War. Except this time, it won't be a few states against the government or the ruling class—it will be all of them."

My head was spinning. Did I hear that right? Our own government, those duly elected public servants, attacked us in our own land? How could that happen? Something was nagging at me though.

"Mike, how were they able to recall the troops and contact the UN for assistance? The EMP took out the whole power grid, right? Where did they get power to do those things?"

"I can help with that one, Mike." Scott and crew had joined us in the shade. "While the people have been left to cover their own asses in case of an EMP event, our illustrious government has been preparing for something like this for years. They have huge Faraday cages full of electronic equipment, as well as underground bunkers hardened against a pulse like we experienced. The bunkers are full of vehicles, choppers, even planes, though not a lot. Planes take up a lot of space. But any assets that were deployed are fine. Another reason we were recalled. They wanted the equipment we had with us. At least we took some with us when we parted ways."

"So, we the people have been relegated to the nineteenth century, by our own leadership, while those in power are sitting in air-conditioned bunkers with hot running water?" My voice raised an octave or three there at the end.

"Yes, ma'am, that's pretty much it. They never did anything to protect the country, just the government and its assets. Maybe that was by design. That information is above my pay grade."

I was seeing red, and from the looks on the faces around me, the feeling was mutual all around. Except for the soldiers. They seemed slightly nonchalant about the situation. "Doesn't this upset you? Why aren't you guys pissed off like the rest of us?"

Scott gave me a crooked smile. "Because, having served in our country's military, nothing this administration does or says surprises me anymore, ma'am. Then, we had to do what we were ordered to do. Now, we're doing what we think is right. Now is better, for me anyway." His brothers in arms were nodding in agreement.

Dane took a step back, stretched and surveyed the area. "Well, I think we'll do a perimeter sweep and then head back to town to keep an eye on things while you're out here, Sheriff. Unless you have something else you need us to do."

Gary shook his head. "No, that sounds great, fellas. I should be back in a few hours. Thanks again for all your help."

Dane smiled. "You don't have to keep thanking us, sir. This is what we're supposed to do."

****

We relayed the information we had received from the soldiers to the rest of our group over dinner. Shock, anger, even disappointment were the reactions to the news. Monroe was mad enough to spit nails.

"Those bastards! I ain't the least bit surprised to hear it but it still makes me madder than a wet hen. Damn government! All they want is power—power over us and over everything we've got. And they tried shutting off the power to do it!"

The irony of Monroe's statement caused a few snickers, but the mood was decidedly sour through the rest of the meal. The

Thompson brothers were talking quietly amongst themselves. Matt looked at Monroe resolutely.

"Uncle Monroe, me and Nick are thinkin' about joining the militia."

Monroe shook his head. "You can think about it all you want, but you ain't doing it. Not 'til you're eighteen. That's what, six more months for you, Matt? Eighteen months for Nick? I promised your momma if anything happened to them I'd finish raisin' ya. When you turn eighteen, I reckon I'll be done."

Matt looked dejected, Nick even more so. Mike addressed the two teenagers. "Guys, this won't be like signing up for the service. There's no big money backing this movement. Supplies are scavenged from abandoned homes and fallen enemy troops, or donated by the people. Our soldiers brought stuff with them, but things like bullets, bandages, uniforms—those are finite resources. Jeeps run out of gas or get flat tires. The other side will have the resources and our people will be trying to find ways to get them. It's going to get ugly."

Matt lifted his chin. "That's alright. It's worth it for our freedom. I'll stay and wait for Nick. But when he's old enough, we go. Until then, we'll see if we can help the cause by finding some of that stuff for our guys on the front line. We'll start scavenging the area ASAP."

Millie had silent tears run down her cheeks. She reached across the table and took Matt's hand. "Your parents would be so proud of the strong, brave men you are becoming. You will both be great assets to our cause. You've grown up so much just since this started, I hardly recognize the two little boys who used to chase my chickens across the yard and tried to practice bull riding on a cow." We giggled at the image as the boys blushed.

Monroe was cackling. "I plumb forgot about that! That was a sight for sure. Little Nick on old Tess's back, Matt whackin' her in the butt with a switch and her just moseyin' along wondering what the hell was going on."

Now we were all rolling with laughter. Even Ryan, who seemed to be finding his smile more and more, joined in. Jabbing Nick with his elbow, he grinned and said, "Now that's a sight I would have liked to have seen. Care to recreate it for us? Only this time, let's use a real bull. Titan's been riding every cow on the place; time for him to get rode. Let me go see if I can catch him …"

Nick's eyes got big, then he realized Ryan was teasing him and he returned the grin. "You first, Ryan." Ryan threw his head back, laughing hard and loud. Oh my. To see him like that, no sign of the pain and anger on his face, made the day not suck quite as bad.

"I think that's a great idea, Matt. The scavenging, not the bull riding." Mike winked as he said it. "I'll try to catch Dane at the gardens in the next day or so and let him know. I'm sure they are building a network to share information and resources. There will be militia teams everywhere. Nothing will go to waste."

"What can we do to help, Mike? Surely, we can donate some stuff we have extras of around here. Do we have any idea what supplies are needed?" I asked.

"Since they brought a lot with them, they'll probably be set for a while, but I'll ask if there are any immediate needs. The longer this lasts, the greater the need will be for help from the citizens. And just to let everyone know, at some point I'll be leaving to join the militia as well."

I didn't know what to say. Apparently neither did anyone else because silence engulfed the dinner table. Mike was leaving us? He had become such an integral part of our family. Almost every improvement to security had been either his idea or built by him. He had started on the solar and wind setup for power to the house. How could he leave?

Monroe was the voice of reason. "Well, Mike, I can't say I'm surprised. Our boys will need experienced leaders. I reckon you'd do more good out there than holed up in here. Hell, if I was thirty years younger, I might join ya."

Mike looked at Monroe and raised an eyebrow. "Thirty years?"

The older man squinted back at him. "Yeah, smartass. Even close to fifty I coulda kicked some UN ass."

The tension from Mike's announcement broken, we began talking amongst ourselves. Russ leaned over to Mike and asked quietly, "How long until you leave?"

"I'm going to finish the power setup for sure. I kind of want to wait and let them get everyone situated first. Dane's group didn't find their way here by accident. Along with the assistance they are providing the sheriff, they are scouting the area looking for good spots to set up camps and keeping an eye out for any UN or DHS entities in the area. Being this far from a major city is a plus. It will take them a while to get to everyone in the rural areas. Hopefully by then we'll have the upper hand. Plus, they apparently have a problem with losing those door-to-door teams."

Russ looked at him confused. "Losing them? Are they defecting?"

Mike gave him a sly grin. "More like disappearing. They just never make it back. No sign of them, their weapons, their vehicles, nothing. At first, search parties were sent out to find them, but after a couple of those never got back, they stopped looking. I guess they consider them collateral damage."

Monroe chimed in, "More like pig food somewhere. Nice of them fellas to donate their guns to the cause though."

Sara looked at Lee. "Pig food?"

Lee shook his head at her. "You don't want to know."

****

After Mike talked to Dane, we started gathering clothes and boots, sheets and blankets, and we set aside some ammo. It wasn't a lot, since we didn't want our own stores to be depleted but we also had reloading equipment and supplies. Russ told Mike if the guys would police their brass and bring it to us, we would reload as long as we had the stuff to do it. They said they'd be happy to do it.

Mike stepped up his work on the solar and wind power setups. It felt like he was trying to hurry it up so he could leave us. As much as I wanted the power to be on in any capacity, that chore being done could signal Mike's departure from our family. I wasn't sure if the tradeoff was worth that. I told him as much.

"Do you really have to go, Mike? I mean, if all of our troops are back here and fighting the enemy, why do you have to join them?" Yes, I was being selfish.

He looked up from the controller he was hooking up and smiled at me. "Because not too long ago I took an oath to uphold and defend the Constitution against all enemies foreign and domestic. That oath doesn't have an expiration date. Our country is at war with its own government and entities it is in cahoots with to destroy our freedom and our way of life. I have already been trained and can help with the battle. I can be an asset out there."

"But you're an asset here! You know that, right? We need you, too!"

Mike shook his head. "Not as much as those fighting men do, Anne. They need seasoned veterans to help. According to Dane,

249

there are quite a number of troops in the militia that were still in boot camp when everything went down. They need help to finish their training. I'll be back when I can. You can't get rid of me that easy," he said with a teasing tone.

I went to him and hugged him fiercely. As I leaned back and looked him in the eye with tears streaming down my face, I replied, "You damn well better come back as often as possible. You will always have a home here. Always."

He smiled again, his eyes shining. "Thank you, Anne. I've tried to imagine what my life would have been like if I hadn't met you all. I would probably have made it for a while, but one man alone wouldn't last long in this world, not the way it is now. That's one of the reasons I have to go. They did this to us. They turned our lives upside down. They can't get away with that. I need to do what I can to make them pay and secure our freedom. I *will* come back. I promise."

I hugged him again, then walked away, tears still falling. War was here, whether we liked it or not.

Chapter 17

Alan and crew had walked a couple of miles from where they stashed the trucks to the Thompson place. Silas was wheezing like a three pack a day smoker as they got to the driveway. "I … don't … think … I … can … go … any … farther …" he managed to get out before collapsing to the ground. The group of men stood there staring at him lying on the ground gasping for breath. After a moment, Alan barked, "Well don't just stand there. Help Tubby get up. We'll take five on the back porch over there." He motioned to the house. "We'll decide who's going where once we get inside while we wait for him to either catch his breath or keel over."

Two of them grabbed Silas by the arms and pretty much dragged him across the yard. They dropped him on the bottom step, where he fell over still gasping for air. Les laughed. "You look like a big fat fish that jumped out of the bowl, sucking air." Les's men laughed. Alan didn't, so neither did Steve or Rich. Alan addressed the group.

"Yeah, funny. Look, when we get in there, we're going to need to get everybody in place as fast as we can. We'll split up. Half goes left, half goes right. Two at the back, two in the middle, two at the front on each side. Once everybody's in place, we attack."

"How will we know when everybody's in place?" Les asked.

"The ones in front start shooting. If they don't, I'll find them and shoot them myself," Alan replied. "I'll start in the back and work my way toward the house. You want middle or front?"

"I'll take the middle. Maybe we can take the house fast."

Alan nodded. "Cool. Who you got you trust to start shooting up front?"

Doug raised his hand. "I'll take the front. I don't give a shit about any of these people. They can all rot in hell for all I care."

Alan grinned. "Good for you. Guess you figured out there ain't too many people left in the world you can trust."

Doug had a hate-filled look on his face. "The whole town shunned me after they found out I took the food from the school. Screw 'em all."

With that settled, they set out for the former clearing to gain entry to the farm. The battle was about to begin.

****

They seemed to be coming from every direction. How was that possible? How did they get through the overgrowth without us knowing? But then again, maybe they all came in from the back and spread out before they got to the house. It was that time of the evening when the dusky dark plays tricks on your eyes. We had tried to stay on alert since Gary had told us about possible trouble from them. There was gunfire coming from the fence line behind the campers, the front by the gate, the back side of the barn, and the house. The house! The kids! Millie!

I practically leapt from the tree house overlook, shouting for Russ. "Russ! They're at the house! Millie is there with the children! I'm on my way! Send back up! Nothing here is worth dying over except for the people in that house!"

He yelled back, "Go! Matt and Nick should be right behind you! I'll be there as soon as I can!"

I nodded and kept running as fast I could. My mind was racing with all the horrible scenarios that could possibly await me when I got there. Tears were streaming down my face making it hard to see. I stumbled over rocks and tree roots that seemed to jump out in front of me, as if they were trying to slow my progress. My son, my only son, was in that house, trying to grab a nap before his sentry duty in a few hours. He would have heard the shots. He would be rushing headlong toward them, toward the danger. Oh God, please keep him safe!

As I got close to the house, I heard crying and shouting—crying from the kids and shouting from unknown male voices. I didn't think I could run any faster, but it certainly felt like I picked up some speed. Just as I rounded the corner, I heard a bone-chilling scream. It came from Rusty.

****

"Look old lady, just let us in! I hear kids in there, hollerin'. You don't want nothin' to happen to them, do ya? Just put the gun down and chill the fuck out. We just want your supplies. Nobody gotta die over some tuna and jerky."

The man who had spoken appeared to be the leader. Millie wasn't impressed. "The only supplies you're getting from this house is some double ought buckshot if you get anywhere near this door. You'd best clear out before I decide to give you some."

The man yelled back from behind the tree, "That's how you wanna play it? Fine! Let's dance, bitch!"

He pointed a pistol at her and started firing. Millie stepped back inside the doorway and shut the old, heavy, solid wood door. She could hear bullets hitting the door and was thankful at that moment there was no window in it. That's how doors were made back when the house was built. Still, she instinctively flinched as each one hit and stepped back away from it. Thank goodness he was out as far as he was. She hoped she could keep him there.

Rusty skidded around the corner from the stairs. "Are you alright, Aunt Millie? Are you hit? How many are there?"

She turned to him with a concerned look. "I'm fine, child. I don't know how many there are. I only heard and saw one, but I also heard a good deal of gunfire so …"

"Okay, you head down to the basement with the little kids and I'll—"

"I'll do no such thing. Right now, you and I are the only thing between those marauders and our home. Until someone gets up here to help, I will be right here with you. I—"

The sound of breaking glass preempted the look of shock on Millie's face. She looked down and saw a bright red spot spreading across her abdomen. The shot through the kitchen window had surprised her since there were some thin curtains over it. It was easy to overlook a weak spot when you couldn't see out well. She dropped the shotgun as she went to her knees with both hands on her stomach. Rusty rushed to her side and yelled, "Aunt Millie! No! No! Kate! Carrie! Somebody—help!" He laid his rifle down and put his own hands on her wound in an attempt to stop the bleeding, tears streaming down his face.

Millie looked into his eyes and smiled. "There, there, honey. It's okay. I know what's waiting for me and I'm ready. Tell everyone I love them. Tell Monroe he was my life. You'll tell him that for me, won't you, dear?"

As her eyes closed and she slumped against the wall, Rusty laid his head on the shoulder of the only grandmother he had ever really known and released a keening wail. "Nooooooooo!"

****

I stopped at the tree closest to the front door as bullets whizzed past me. I stooped down behind the tree trying to make myself as small a target as possible. Staying where I was while hearing my son's cry was one of the hardest things I had ever done. Just as I thought to myself, *The hell with it, that's my baby in there and I'm going*, Matt and Nick ran up behind me.

Matt whispered in my ear, "We'll distract them. I'll tell you when to go."

I nodded, every muscle in my body poised to spring me toward the house as soon as he said the word. They both looked around the tree, which immediately sent shots our way. They ducked and looked at each other.

"You got yours, Nick?" Matt asked of his brother.

"Got him. You go left, I'll go right." Nick checked his rifle. Matt did the same.

"On three. One. Two. Three! Go now, Anne!" Matt stood as he said it and fired wildly in the direction of the incoming rounds earlier. When there was no return fire, I took off like a relay racer. I hit the middle step and was in the front door in another two steps. I slammed it behind me and screamed for my son.

"Rusty! Rusty, where are you?" I tore through the living room into the dining room screaming his name.

"In here, Mom! Hurry!"

I found him in the kitchen with Millie, just as Kate and Carrie came rushing through the door from the basement, each with their homemade medic kits, and Carrie with a rifle slung over her shoulder.

Kate's hand flew to her mouth as she saw Millie. She quickly knelt down and put three fingers to Millie's neck, checking her carotid artery for a pulse. There was none. She turned to Carrie with tears in her eyes and said quietly, "She's gone. Please go back to the kids, keep them safe. You're a much better shot than me and you're in no shape to be running around out there. I'll stay up here in case we have any injuries."

Carrie nodded, kissed her fingertips and placed them on Millie's forehead, then headed back downstairs with tears flowing. Kate looked at me and asked softly, "Is anyone else hurt?"

I was numb. I was definitely in shock. I stared at Millie's body lying on the floor of her kitchen. How could she be gone? She was our mother, grandmother, aunt, sister—so many things all rolled into one wonderful person. She still had so much to teach us. Who would show us the old ways she hadn't gotten to yet? How would Monroe go on without her? Monroe. He was at the barn. He could have heard Rusty's screams coming from the house. He would be trying to make his way here to her to make sure she was alright.

"I don't know yet. I haven't heard. I need to find Monroe. He'll try to get here, to her. We don't know where all these people are. It's dangerous to be anywhere outside."

Rusty knelt next to me, back straight, face resolute. "I'll go, Mom. You may be needed here to protect the kids. I'll find Monroe and get him back here safe."

I looked at him like he had grown a third arm. "You most certainly will not! It's dangerous out there! You're a kid, too! You're *my* kid! No!"

He smiled a sad smile at me. "I'm sixteen, Mom. I'm not a kid anymore, not in this world. We've been training in case something like this happened. I can help out there. There's nothing I can do in here." He looked down at Millie's still form. "Besides, it's dangerous in here, too. You guys keep your heads down. See if you can find something to cover that window with and douse the lanterns. I'll be back with Monroe as quick as I can."

Without waiting for my permission or a response, my not-so-little boy ran hunched down below the windows toward the front door. I looked at the spot I had last seen him in. *When did it happen? When did my son become a man?* I cursed whoever had put us in this situation that robbed my son of the last few years of his childhood. As if sensing my tortured thoughts, Kate laid a hand on my shoulder.

"He's smart, Anne. He's as well trained as he can be. He'll make it back, I know it. Here, help me get Millie covered up and let's see if we can find something to cover that window."

As if in a trance, I let Kate lead me to the cupboard that held our biggest cookie sheets. We pulled two out and placed them side by side, which covered most of the window. We blew out the lantern and plunged the kitchen into darkness. I automatically pulled a flashlight from my pocket and handed it to her. She led the way to the linen closet in the hall and pulled out a sheet. We laid it gently over Millie's body and hugged each other as we cried our sorrow at losing such a wonderful soul in such a brutal way. She was supposed to die peacefully in her sleep in ten or twenty years, after the world stopped being crazy and we had something akin to normal back. She didn't deserve this.

I pulled away from Kate as a thought hit me. "What did you mean about Carrie being in no condition to be running around outside? What's wrong with her?"

Kate smiled the smile of a woman with a secret. "Carrie's pregnant. We just found out this morning, thanks to your forethought of stocking pregnancy tests. She hasn't even told Ryan yet, so please don't tell anyone else until she gets a chance to tell him."

Voice full of dread, I replied, "Pray she gets a chance to tell him."

****

Ryan was in the tree house crouched behind the sheet metal wall. Shots had been fired toward the area but nothing as high as he was. He hoped they didn't know about the overlook as it would give him a distinct advantage in the fight. The sun was sinking fast and visibility was rapidly going to shit. He scanned the area with the night vision monocular we had brought with us and spied one of the marauders creeping along the tree line. He used a couple of large bushes as a focal point to target where the man was. He let the monocular drop to hang from the lanyard around his neck and set his target location through his scope. He fired a single shot, ejected the spent casing and quickly pulled the monocular back up. The man had stopped and seemed to be holding his side. Ryan sighted the approximate location of his head, and shot again. His third look through night vision showed a body lying on the ground, not moving. Ryan smiled to himself then felt a moment of … he wasn't sure what it was, but it wasn't pride or satisfaction. *What's wrong with me? This is it, this is what I've been waiting for—payback for Bill.* He paused, in awe of the new emotions running through him. His next thought was of Carrie. He worried that she was in danger and he wasn't there to protect her. At that moment, he realized that his need for vengeance for his brother's murder was now outweighed and overshadowed by his love for Carrie. She had become the most important thing in his life and he wanted, no needed to live, for her; to find out where the future would take them. He definitely wanted to know how it all turned out.

With this realization on his mind, he wanted nothing more than to go to her and make sure she was alright. To do that, he had to help his family clear their home of the uninvited guests who were wreaking havoc everywhere. He started scanning for more targets. With Bob and Russ in the foxholes, the three of them cleared the front gate area in short order. Even without night vision, the muzzle flashes from the scavengers gave them a good idea of where they were located. The shots didn't have to be kill shots. These guys pretty much dropped out of the fight when they got hit.

Mike had been canvassing the back section of the property looking for any weak spots when he heard the shooting. Running toward the sound, he called over the radio. "Sitrep!" Everyone knew that was short for situation report. The devil dog had taught us some military lingo, which we could use without feeling like we were dishonoring vets who had actually fought for the right to use it.

Russ was the first to respond. "Quiet at the gate now. Looks like we had three unfriendlies. They are no longer firing, but we have not confirmed they are dead yet. We'll give it a few more minutes and verify. I'll let you know for sure."

Mike keyed back. "Roger that. Jim?"

Jim replied, "Campground is under attack! House is under attack! Shots fired at the house! There's at least three different groups coming at us! We need help up here!"

Mike answered, "We're on our way, Jim! Russ, one of you guys head back, too! And be careful where you shoot—everybody looks the same in the dark."

Russ responded, "Will do. Give us a minute to check these guys."

Overhearing Jim's frantic call, Ryan scrambled out of the tree house. He ran to the foxhole Russ was in and handed him the monocular. "I'm heading to the house. I'd say give it five minutes, check those guys for life then one of you head back, too. After another five, if there's no activity, leave this and come back, whichever of you is left."

Russ gave him a grim nod. "Keep your head down, Ryan. Don't take any chances. Be safe."

Ryan shot back a quick grin. "Mr. Safety, that's me. I got my head on straight, Russ. I plan to keep my head and the rest of my body intact. You guys stay safe, too." He held his fist up to Russ, who obliged him with a bump. Ryan took off for the house, running as fast as he could while staying as low as possible.

Russ called over to Bob. "Did you see that? I think he's back. I think the old Ryan has come home."

Bob grinned a slight grin that Russ couldn't see in the falling darkness, but could hear in his voice. "I did, and it's about damn time. I missed that little piss-ant."

"Me, too, buddy. Now let's go see if these douche bags are out of the fight so we can get to our families. If anything has happened to any of our people, none of these assholes are getting out of here alive."

****

Monroe was in the barn with Luke and Brian when the shooting started. Ben was in the loft on watch. Monroe yelled up to him as he brought his rifle around. "Ben! What's going on out there? Can you see anything?"

Ben had a pair of binoculars but with the waning light his vision was limited. "A little bit, Uncle Monroe. I can see people down there, and the flashes from the guns going off. Should I come down?"

As Monroe was about to speak, the interaction between Jim and Mike came over the radio Lee was holding. Luke started for the door but Monroe grabbed his arm. "Hold on, son. Don't run off half-cocked."

Luke jerked his arm away. "Casey is alone in our camper! The door won't even be locked! I have to go, Monroe!"

"I understand that; I've got a wife over there, too. Let's just make sure we get to them in one piece. Okay?"

Luke paused, took a breath, and looked Monroe in the eye. "Fine. How do we get over there then?"

Monroe pulled his rifle up and held it out to Luke. "This scope has a night vision setting. You've got younger eyes than me, so take it over to the door, open it a crack and see if you can see anybody. But don't shoot! Remember what Mike said. Verify first."

Luke took the proffered gun and hurried to the barn door. Staying as close to the wall as possible, he pulled it up and scanned the area. "I see at least six guys in all; two by the house, two behind the bunkhouse, and two ... at the campers! One of them is about to open the door to my camper!"

Just as he was about to click the safety off the rifle, in the hopes he could hit the man from there, he saw whoever was trying to enter his camper shoot backwards to the ground after a flash of light and the unmistakable sound of a shotgun blast. He watched in awe as the door closed and the light inside was extinguished.

"Holy shit! She shot him! She blew him away!" Luke turned to Monroe and Brian with a big grin on his face. "My woman is bad ass!"

Monroe laughed at him. "All of our women are bad ass. Why, if that had been my Millie, she would have—"

Just then, Rusty ran through the barn door. "Uncle Monroe! Aunt Millie! She's ..." He stopped, unable to tell the beloved old man that his wife was gone.

He didn't have to. Monroe knew by the look in his eye. "What? Millie? My Millie's dead? No, no, you're wrong, boy. She's fine. I'll just go check on her."

Rusty stood in front of Monroe with tears streaming down his face. "She's gone. Kate checked. Someone shot her through the kitchen window. I'm sorry, Uncle Monroe, I wasn't able to protect her." He was crying so hard now he couldn't speak clearly.

Monroe's face was unreadable. "Did she say anything, before she … died?"

Rusty nodded. "She said to tell everyone that she loved them. And to tell you that you were her life. I'm so sorry."

Monroe ruffled Rusty's hair. "It's not your fault, son. But somebody's gonna pay for this. Now."

He reached out his hand to Luke, who turned the rifle over to its owner. He checked the breach to make sure the round he already knew was there still was, and walked out the barn door. Brian yelled for him to wait, but he couldn't be heard over the angry shouting. "You bastards killed my wife, the sweetest woman to ever walk the face of this God forsaken earth! None of you will leave here alive! You hear me? You're all dead, you just don't know it yet! C'mon, you thievin', murderin', good-for-nothin' cowards! What, are you afraid of an old man? Come out from behind them bushes so I can—"

Two shots rang out, one from outside the screen porch at the back corner of the house, the other from the side of the bunkhouse.

Monroe might have lived through one of them, but not both. He fell to the ground as Matt was taking out the shooter behind the house. He had snuck around to get the drop on the guy. When Monroe started yelling, he knew he had the distraction he needed and was taking aim to fire when the guy shot Monroe. The shot startled Matt, but he quickly calmed himself enough to finish the man.

At the same time, Mike was coming in from the back field, Sean right behind, having already downed two invaders themselves. He saw the muzzle flash from outside the bunkhouse, and watched in horror as Monroe crumpled to the ground. Without hesitation, he drew a bead on the spot he had seen the flash originate from and fired until his breach locked open from the spent magazine, running to Monroe the whole time. He slid in beside him and pressed his hands to the wounds on his chest. He looked down at him and whispered fiercely, "Don't you die on me, soldier. I haven't given you permission to die!"

Monroe coughed, blood seeping from his mouth, "I don't reckon I asked for your permission, jarhead. You take care of these people. They're good folks. Some of the best I've ever known. It was an honor to know you, Marine. I gotta go now. My Millie is waiting for me. I see her smiling, holding her hand out to me ..."

Monroe stopped breathing. Mike checked for a pulse, knowing he wouldn't find one. He gently closed Monroe's eyes, leaned his head back and howled his rage.

****

Alan was hiding behind the old outhouse, watching his crew fall. He didn't hear any more shots from the front, which meant Rich, Doug, and Junior were dead. Steve had been blown away by that bitch in the camper. Les never came out from behind the barn so he was obviously a goner, along with his new sidekick, Silas. *Hell, that whiny bitch probably ran back home when the shooting started with piss running down his legs. Wanted the goods, but didn't have the guts to get them.* The rest of Les's crew lay where they had fallen around the yard. *At least I got that old bitch through the window. That's what she gets for not letting us in, letting us have the goods. Now I just gotta figure out how to get outta here.*

He was looking around behind him for a path of some kind he could use to get away without being seen. He turned back toward the house to see a man standing there with a pistol aimed at his forehead. He started to raise his own sidearm when the man pulled the hammer back on his gun.

"Don't even think about it. What, did you think you were going to slink off into the night after what you people have done here? No, you'll be dropping that gun, putting your hands up, and coming with me."

"The hell I will! You want to stop me? You're gonna have to shoot me!" Alan raised his gun.

267

"Fine. Have it your way. Rot in hell." The man fired point blank into Alan's face.

****

Lee had been watching from the bunkhouse window, where he had been working on a rough piece of wood that needed sanding. He was just finishing up when the shooting started. He rushed to the door with his pistol drawn, but couldn't see well and didn't want to hit one of his own people. He retreated back into the darkness of the bunkhouse and crouched below a window. He saw the marauder yell at Millie to let them in and let them have the supplies. He watched in horror as the evil man stepped back, walked over to the kitchen window and fired a shot inside. He heard him laughing as he ran to hide behind the outhouse. After the hail of gunfire ceased, he opened the door and crept to the side of the outhouse. He raised his gun and rounded the corner. After he shot him, he calmly walked back out into the yard and toward the house, even though his hands were shaking. He needed to check on his family—Aiden and Moira, and Sara and Tony.

****

Ryan ran toward the house just in time to see Monroe fall. He skidded to a stop and looked for hostiles. After two more shots from the other side of the house, things got quiet. No more shooting, just the sounds of anguish coming from Mike. He yelled out, "Sitrep!" He received a "Clear!" from the back of the house that sounded like Matt. Another came from the outhouse. Lee? Brian called it from the barn, Jim from the campground. Russ and Bob ran up behind him.

"Is everyone okay? Has anyone been to the house? What's—" Russ stopped, able to see the body in the last remnants of the sunlight. He couldn't tell who it was, so he rushed over to the spot. He found Mike, still on his knees with Monroe's head in his lap. Bob was right on Russ's heels. Seeing his uncle lying there, he dropped down beside him.

"What? Why?" The shock was evident in his tone.

Mike shook his head. "I don't know. I got here and heard him yelling, but I couldn't hear what he was saying. He walked right out in the open. Why would he do that?"

Brian and Rusty joined the group. Brian told them what had happened to Millie. Bob was overcome with grief and cried silent tears. He gave himself a moment, then rose to his feet, wiping his face. "I've gotta go find Janet. She's gonna be torn apart by this—losing both of them at the same time."

He got to his feet and turned toward the house. Mike looked up at him. "Announce yourselves. They're going to be jumpy in there."

Bob nodded and headed off, Russ beside him. Looking straight ahead, he said, "This is gonna be bad, real bad. Janet and Anne ..." He didn't finish the thought.

Russ wiped his own tears away. "Yes, it is, buddy. It sure is."

****

We could hear Janet's scream from the basement. She flew up the stairs, Marietta right behind, weapon drawn.

"Aunt Millie? Aunt Millie! Where is she?" As she came through the door, she saw the sheet draped over her aunt's body, a blood-soaked section in the center. She fell to the floor beside her beloved aunt, sobbing uncontrollably. "This is all my fault! I was the one who suggested bugging out here. We made them a target! If we hadn't come here—"

I put my arm around her shoulders. "It wouldn't have mattered whether we were here or not, honey. They would have been found, probably a lot sooner without the fortifications we put in place. And if we weren't here, those people would have taken this place over. Do you think Millie would have rather that happened? You

270

know she wouldn't. I know how bad you're hurting, Janet. I know—"

"How do you know?" She lashed out at me hatefully as she jerked away. "This woman was like a mother to me! Who did you lose that you loved today?"

I reached down under the sheet and pulled Millie's cool hand into mine. I looked at Janet with tear-filled eyes. "Her."

Janet broke down again. "Oh, Anne, I'm sorry. I didn't mean to take it out on you. I love you, you know that. It just hurts so bad …"

I put my arm around her again. "I know, sweetie, I know. We'll get through this, together. All of us."

At that moment, Russ called from the porch. "We're coming in. Don't shoot!"

He and Bob came through the doorway and saw the devastation left behind from a senseless act of violence. Russ pulled me up to him as Bob joined his wife on the floor beside Millie. We both cried ourselves out into the strong shoulders of our husbands. Kate and Marietta were supporting each other as well.

Sara and Carrie came to the top of the stairs and peeked around the corner. Sara asked, "Is it safe to come up? The children are really scared and need to see their parents."

I lifted my head and looked at Russ. He nodded and said, "Yes, I think we're clear, but make sure they stay inside the house. We'll get the parents to them."

Bob turned Janet's face up so he could look her in the eye. "Sugar, I've gotta tell you something, and on top of losing Millie, it's gonna be real hard for you to hear."

"Oh, Lord, what else happened? Is Ben okay? Where is he?"

"Yes, Ben's fine. He's still on watch in the loft. No, this is about Monroe." He stopped, giving her a moment to grasp what he was about to say.

She grabbed his arm as her knees buckled. "Nooooo! Please, God, no! Not both of them at the same time!"

He held her close as they cried their sorrow out together. There wasn't a dry eye in the house as the knowledge that the matriarch and patriarch of our home had been taken from us by greed and a complete disregard for human life. Mike came in, followed by the rest of our people.

"I think we're clear. I did a quick sweep with Matt and Nick. No signs of anyone else. We need something to cover Monroe. If you'll tell me where …"

I moved out of Russ's embrace. "I'll get you one. One sec."

I came back with the sheet to find Lee embracing his children, along with Sara and Tony. Marietta and Brian, Carrie and Ryan, Jim and Charlotte, Ashley and her daughter, Shannon, and Luke and Casey all supporting each other in our time of grief. I handed the sheet to Mike and hugged him. "Thank you for helping to keep us safe."

He shook his head. "Not everybody. We lost two people."

I looked around the kitchen at my extended family. I turned back to Mike with a sad smile. "And saved of all these. If it weren't for you and your knowledge and experience, this would have been a lot worse."

Russ joined us, with Rusty under his arm. "She's right, Mike. Without you we wouldn't have been trained to deal with a situation like what we had tonight. Yes, we lost two—but we saved two dozen. I think that's something to be thankful for. Regular people like us can't expect there to be no casualties when we're attacked. We did our best and we won. The bad guys came and they lost. I think Monroe and Millie would be proud of us."

Mike nodded. "They were."

Epilogue

Ryan ran across the yard, chasing his children. "I'm gonna get you, Billy Millie!"

His three-year-old daughter stopped, turned, placed her hands on her hips, and scolded him. "No, Daddy! Just my name! Just Millie! He Billy! I Millie!" She pointed at her twin brother, then looked back at her father with a pout.

He laughed and scooped them both up, making them squeal with delight. "Fine, Millie Jean. Billy *and* Millie. Better?"

She wrapped her chubby arms around his neck. "Better, Daddy. Down! Tickles!"

She tried to wiggle away from the beard he was sporting. He put them both down. Billy ran off after a chicken and Millie ran to her mother on the porch, nursing her newborn baby brother. She peeked inside the blanket.

"Mo eating?"

Carrie smiled at her daughter. "Yes, honey Monroe is eating. Go fetch your brother. It's almost lunchtime."

"K, Mommy."

She went to find her brother as Ryan walked up. Looking over his shoulder to make sure the kids were out of earshot, he looked at his wife with a wicked leer. "Hey, when he's done, how about some for Daddy?"

She swatted at him. "Ryan Lawton, you bad man! You would take your son's food?"

He dodged her swat. "Honey, I'm pretty sure there's enough there to feed a few kids."

She stood up then to try to connect her swing with his arm. He jumped off the porch backwards, laughing and running after his kids. Carrie shook her head, giggled at her lascivious husband, and turned to go inside. She saw Bob standing there with a big grin and she turned fifty shades of red. He laughed then.

"Ah, it's alright, Carrie girl. Just means he loves you. You saved him, you know. You brought him back from the dark place. Not sure he would have made it without you."

She turned to look back at her family. "We saved each other. I didn't think I'd ever find someone I could stand long enough to live the rest of my life with. He makes me laugh every day. He makes me feel loved every minute of every day. Who would have thought it would take the world we knew coming to an end for us to find one another? I guess you could say we needed the dark to see the light."

Bob looked at her with a serious expression. "Damn, girl, that's some deep shit right there." He held the serious look for a second, then smiled. They both laughed as he held the door for her to come inside. "Since you ain't sharin' Mo's food, lunch is ready."

She smacked Bob on the arm. "You too?"

"Ow!" He rubbed his arm as he followed her in the door. "Man, marriage gives women some wicked aim."

She replied over her shoulder, "Husbands give wives a reason to need it."

"Well, yeah, there's that."

****

Sara moaned as the next contraction hit her. Their small cabin was heating up with Kate, Carrie, Lee, and pretty much everyone else either inside or standing in the doorway. Kate stood up and yelled, "If you are not directly responsible or involved in this birth, we need some room! Everybody but Carrie and Lee, out! Oh, and Sara."

There were snickers and laughs as everyone filed out. The cabins had been built close to the house so they could tie into the septic tank. It was closing in on five years since the power had gone off. There were no new updates as to when—or even if—it would come back on. There was fighting across the country, mostly in the larger metropolitan areas between militias and the UN. When we found out our own government had turned out the lights, the people rose up from coast to coast to fight the invading force of the UN and consequently, DHS.

Matt and Nick had left to join the militia unit based out of Nashville, along with Mike. Quite a few of the younger men from town joined up as well, including Clay Glass. That was a shocker. We didn't think Clay cared about anyone but himself and his momma. Rhonda's wailing could be heard almost to our place, but we heard Clay stood up to her that day.

"Momma, you ain't disabled. You're lazy. You need to get out in the yard and plant some food. I'll get it started for you, but you're gonna have to take care of it if you want to eat. The ladies in town will help you put it up. I'm going to fight for our country, Momma. Jay woulda if he was still here. I need to do this. I love you, Momma, but you don't need me. You need to get up off your butt and do stuff." Yep, Gary got a kick out of telling us that story. We hadn't heard she died, so apparently Rhonda was doing okay by herself. We sure did miss our guys though.

We didn't have to talk too hard to keep Ben and Rusty from joining the fight. Well, okay it wasn't us. It was Shannon and Tate. Shannon grew into a beautiful young woman who swept both Ben and Rusty off their feet without trying. It was touch and go for a while there—the boys starting fighting over stupid stuff and we all knew why. Rusty was less aggressive though and when he saw the light in his best friend's eye when the girl walked into a room, he backed off. Ben and Shannon were married soon after they turned eighteen and had a fat little boy two years later they named Pete with Sara's blessing. About a month later, Ashley announced that she was leaving us to live with Tim Miller. We were all in shock, none more so than Charlotte and Jim, since no one knew they were that serious, but we wished her well. She came out to visit about once a month and seemed happy.

Rusty met Tate at the Dotson farm not long after Ben and Shannon were married. He was really contemplating joining the militia and I laid awake many nights in fear that I would lose him after everything we had been through to survive. The day he met her, he came back with a gleam in his eye I hadn't seen since he thought he was in love with Shannon. He was so excited to tell me about her that evening, and I told Russ that night, "I think we just dodged a bullet. Literally." From that point forward, they were together every moment they could find. Tate moved to the farm about a month later, taking the sewing room that had been designated for single gals. Marietta and Brian had moved into their own cabin by then. Two months after that, they said they wanted to get married. Rusty and Ben built a duplex cabin of sorts, and the two couples were together all the time. No grandbabies for me, but no hurry. *No seriously, get busy you two.* I need grandbabies.

With no birth control, babies were popping up everywhere. I mean think about it. No television to watch, no movies to go to, no bowling leagues, nothing that could be considered leisure activities that required electricity were done anymore. We set up a horseshoe pit and a cornhole game. We had croquet and badminton, as well as board games that had seen better days. But when night came, after working hard all day on food and laundry and security and living, we didn't want to do much else but go to bed. See where this is going?

My labor and delivery with Rusty was bad, really bad. We both almost died. After the C-section, the doctor told me I shouldn't have any more. We were heartbroken, but Russ was adamant that my life was more important than another child. So, I'd had my tubes tied. We didn't have anything to worry about. No more babies for me. Kate had had her tubes tied as well.

At twenty-eight, Janet had an abnormal pap smear come back as pre-cancer. She'd had a partial hysterectomy which took care of the problem and kept her from having any more children. Charlotte was past her childbearing years. All the rest of the women were not.

Casey had gotten pregnant about a year after the power went off. In her fifth month, she'd started hemorrhaging. She lost the baby but Kate saved her life. Doc Hanson came out and checked her the next day. He congratulated Kate on a job well done, and gave the Callens the sad news that they likely wouldn't have any children. So far, he was right.

Marietta never got pregnant. She'd told us that her doctor had told her years earlier she probably wouldn't because she had sustained damage after an abortion at sixteen, and the scar tissue would likely not hold an egg. She and Brian were happy together, just the two of them, so we were happy for them. She was always available to babysit, possibly living vicariously through everyone else's babies.

Sara and Lee were married not too long after the attack. Lee said life was too short to play games and he wanted to make her his wife before anything else happened. We didn't think there would be any babies from them after a couple of years, but Sara finally got pregnant. She was close to forty, so Kate had kept a very close eye on her during the pregnancy.

We heard a scream, long and sustained. Janet and I looked at each other. "It's coming!" We all watched the door of the cabin, waiting for the news. After a few minutes, the door opened, and Lee stood there, sweat on his forehead but a smile so wide it didn't seem like his face could hold it.

"It's a girl!" We all jumped up and down and hugged each other.

I looked at Lee. "Are they okay? Both of them?"

He nodded, the grin never waning. "Yes. Sara is fine, tired but fine. The baby is beautiful, ten fingers, ten toes. Kate said she guessed her to weigh close to eight pounds."

My eyes grew wide. "Wow, big girl. Have you picked out a name yet?"

A hint of moisture and sadness touched his eyes as he replied, "Her name is Jackie."

****

The farm wasn't the same after the loss of Millie and Monroe. We buried them on the hill by Pete and Bill, as they had requested so many years ago. For as long as I had been going there, they were a part of the place. They were "the farm." It was hard seeing their things in the house, around the yard, even in Monroe's junk sheds, knowing they were no longer with us to use them. His chair was left vacant in the living room for a long time. Finally, Bob walked over to it during a family meeting and sat down. Voice full of emotion, he said, "Monroe didn't like anything to go to waste. I'm sure he'd want us to use it." From that point forward, the men made a game of trying to get Monroe's seat when we had a get-together inside. No one moved into their bedroom. After a time, we put the bed in Ryan and Carrie's cabin, and set the ham up in its place. It was still our link to the world outside of our town, but we didn't really monitor it throughout the day. We used it get information about how things were going in the war, always hoping to catch a mention of one our people who were out there fighting for our freedom.

We tried to replicate Millie's fresh bread, but we never got it exactly right. Janet did her proud on biscuits and my cornbread was pretty close. Charlotte took over as head canner and continued to teach the younger ones this priceless task. Even with all the people we had, our gardens produced well, our flocks and herds flourished, and we could have lived on what we had put back at any one time for a couple of years.

Our group was growing, mostly by the natural process, and small homes had been built around the main one. Some families chose to have meals at their own homes during the day, but we usually all got together for the evening meal. With multiple kitchens, albeit primitive, we were able to cook different dishes in different places to create a buffet-style dinner. Some cabins had open hearths, some had scavenged wood stoves, some of the women even cooked over open fires outside. We had all developed new ways of doing things we took for granted before. The wood cook stove on the screen porch had been moved inside when the propane was gone. It took some practice, but we got the hang of it. The gas stove had been relegated to the shed, until such time as propane was available again—if it ever was.

We got wind and solar power to the house, enough to run the ceiling fans and lights with low watt CFL bulbs, as well as the refrigerator and a big chest freezer a few hours a day. Mike's "soldier showers," as they had been dubbed, continued to provide us a means to get clean, so my pleas for hot water indoors had been tabled, but hey, we could make ice. Iced tea was back on the menu, and I, for one, had missed it terribly. However, it was now considered a luxury, as the tea bag stores were dwindling. We were drinking instant coffee, which we had stocked up in huge supplies because it lasts almost indefinitely. Yet, without any change in the outside world coming back online any time soon, that too would be gone someday. We had started limiting ourselves to one cup a day. Man, that sucked.

Clothes were worn until we couldn't patch them anymore. Marietta turned out to be a fair seamstress. Sewing was another of Charlotte's gifts. Winters would find both of them, as well as most of the gals, sitting by the fireplace with piles of mending to do. We let some of the men try their hand at it, but they ended up making the hole worse than it had been to begin with. Besides, we liked our girl time. It was a whole lot like a quilting bee without the quilt. We still had some clothing put back, but those stores were diminishing just like everything else. Before joining up, the Thompson boys went on scavenging runs and brought back any clothing they found, no matter the state of the pieces. We sorted through what they brought, washed and dried it, and decided what was salvageable and what would be used as patches, bandages, or for feminine protection. No one ever thinks about running out of those items, but when you do, you have to change the way you do things. Welcome to the past, ladies.

We had adjusted our lives to the world we were left with. This wasn't a new concept. Man has been adapting to his environment as long as he has walked the earth. It's what we do. I won't lie—I missed electricity. I really missed air conditioning and hot running water. I missed settling down with my family and a big bowl of popcorn for movie night, and keeping up with my friends and extended family on social media. I longed for tacos and hamburgers and pizza. Oh, and ice cream with chocolate syrup. I really missed chocolate. We cooked hearty, wholesome, and in large batches. No room for junk food, not that we had any anymore. We had tried our hand at making potato chips. They were a little thick, but man they were awesome. We kept trying and everyone encouraged us to continue. Bob's exact words were, "Keep tryin' 'til ya get it right. I'll keep tastin' for ya and let you know." We had the feeling that, as far as Bob was concerned, that day would never come.

The longed-for luxuries and amenities were nothing we had to have to live our lives. We had built a clan on the farm. A clan of people who cared for and watched out for each other. A tribe that put the needs of the group before themselves. Yes, I had selfish thoughts from time to time—we all did. I wondered if my house was still standing and, if it was, what kind of shape it was in. We never went back to check. What good would it do? We were safer here than there. But I missed it. I missed my little family in our own space. I selfishly longed for my old life. But even if the power came back on tomorrow, it wouldn't be the same. Rusty was grown and had his own family now. That life was gone. I looked around at the people who had become my life—my world—and knew I was right where I was supposed to be.

Sitting under the trees outside the house at the tables that still looked almost as good as the day Lee built them, we oohed and aahed over baby Jackie. The sun was going down and the bats were doing their job at pest control. We were talking and laughing like we always did after dinner as the kids were gathering the dishes to take to the house when everyone stopped dead in their tracks. Not a word was spoken as we all looked toward the driveway.

The yard light had come on.

Acknowledgements

This series has been quite a journey for me. I still find it hard to call myself an author. Maybe I shouldn't yet. Maybe I need ten books under my belt before I could wear that title, or a New York Times bestseller (not gonna happen), or some kind of literary award (again, not gonna happen). Or maybe I just say screw it–I wrote some books, people bought them, so that makes me an author. Yeah, I think I'll work with that.

I made mistakes in my writing which my attentive readers brought to my attention. Thank you if this applies to you. I did not take it personal. I love that you let me know you were paying attention well enough to catch my screw ups. I tried to research when I needed to but didn't if I thought I knew it. Note to self: next time, research more.

Wait, what? Next time? Yes, there will be more from me. I am starting a new series before the end of the year but I am not setting any kind of deadline for when it will be done because apparently, I suck at meeting deadlines. I don't want to give too much away but it will be prepper fiction, just from a different point of view. If you aren't on my mailing list, and you enjoy my work, I encourage you to join so you can get updates about the new series when it's time. You can get there from my website.

Since I went with a publisher, my thank you list will be a bit different this time. First and foremost, my thanks go to my husband. He gives me whatever time I want or need to put the words together. He lets me bounce ideas off him and work out the logistics to make them viable parts of the story. He is my biggest fan and I couldn't have done any of this without him. He read the first words I wrote of this tale and tells me he still loves it. Thank you, baby.

Next, I'd like to thank my advanced reader team. They got on the stick and got me the issues they found in just a couple of days. You guys are amazing and I am very grateful you wanted to be a part of this project.

I want to thank all my readers. The ones who follow my Facebook page; the ones who are on my mailing list; the ones who left reviews, good or bad. You are all a part of this adventure. A writer is nothing if no one buys or reads their books. Thank you for checking in to find out where I was on the last book. Thank you for nagging me to finish it. Thank you for encouraging me to continue when I wondered if what I had written was good enough. I guess it was.

As always, last but in no way least, I want to thank God for the gifts he has given me to entertain you and hopefully make you think about "what if." I give Him all the glory. I placed my life in

His hands and all I have is because of Him. Thank you, Lord, for the many blessings you bestow upon me every day.

Find us on the web!

The website is always updating, so keep coming back for more info. Want to stay up to date on all our latest news? Join our mailing list for updates giveaways and events!

www.paglaspy.com

Facebook: facebook.com/paglaspy

Twitter: @paglaspy

Goodreads: P.A. Glaspy

Bookhub: P.A. Glaspy

23513165R00178

Made in the USA
Columbia, SC
09 August 2018